Night of the Shadow
J. K. Winn

Copyright © by J. K. Winn, jamaxwin@yahoo.com

All rights reserved.

Copying in any amount, in any format, with any device, is prohibited without the express permission of the author, except when used in reviews.

Also by J. K. Winn

Shadow Series
Out of the Shadow
Night of the Shadow

The Spirit Series
The Spirit Keepers
The Spirit Seekers
The Spirit Breakers: A Pueblo People's Mystery

Standalone
River of Desire
The Last Supper: A Short Story
Hold Back the Wind

Table of Contents

Dedicated
To the Women of AA

Table of Contents

Chapter One

Chapter One

Ellie

Sights and sounds swelled around her: The backlit bar and throbbing beat of overhead speakers, the loud voices and hot young bodies, the warm, euphoric sensation of alcohol as it flowed down her esophagus and into her veins. All was as it should be.

Friday night, Happy Hour. Her favorite time of the week. Out with friends at Graffiti Bar, 13th and Market, Downtown Philadelphia.

Jessica busily chatted with a stranger on her far side who had taken their friend Jack's seat at the bar when he wandered off to dance with a blonde. Leaving Ellie out. That would usually bother Ellie, but no matter tonight, she had a full drink, compliments of Jessica's newest admirer, and the alcohol blunted any irritation. She struck up a conversation with the man on her right, who didn't appear interested at all, but they rambled on, incoherently at times, about traffic and transportation, taking a circuitous route through a lengthy dialogue.

That was the last thing she would remember about the night. By the time she awoke under her own down comforter the following morning, all she was left with was a throbbing headache, a desert-dry mouth and no memory of what happened later. Had she left the bar with Jessica? Or gone straight home? She racked her brains trying to recall, but nothing came to mind.

So, when she received the call from Jack telling her Jessica had died...she was as shocked as anyone.

Six weeks later.

"I can't believe I ordered that margarita." Ellie said to her new AA sponsor Maddie, across the table from her at the Queen Village *Starbucks*. Maddie wasn't much older than Ellie, but she had three years of recovery...an eternity where Ellie was concerned. "I should have known better...who am I fooling...I do know better. I don't understand how it could have happened.

Instead of looking at her with the disgust she felt for herself, Maddie wore a sympathetic expression. "Relapses are common, especially early in recovery. I wouldn't beat myself up too much for this one mistake."

"Maybe, but I feel like I unconsciously sabotaged myself. After all these weeks of sobriety, of laughter and joy, of friendship and camaraderie, I'm back in a deep dark hole of alcoholic despair."

"There's something you can do about it."

"I know...but I'm not ready."

"Did you drink today?"

Ellie nodded glumly. "Yeah, I had a couple glasses of chardonnay earlier."

"I thought so."

"And now that I'm drinking again, the flashbacks have returned with a vengeance. I've been having these crazy, disjointed memories of the night Jessica was murdered."

"Murdered? I thought you said the coroner's office had written the death off as accidental. With her drinking, didn't they conclude she fell and hit her head?"

"They did, but these recollections are telling me another story."

"What kind of story?"

"In them, I'm awakened out of a deep sleep by a shockingly loud fight. When I force my eyes open, I spot two people struggling. Although it's not entirely clear, I strongly suspect one of them is Jessica. If that's true, then I can confirm something more heinous than an accident happened to her. It's difficult enough to fathom a mere fall would end Jessica's life, but the idea someone murdered her, and I might have been a witness, is more than I can handle."

"All this has to be terribly unsettling.

"To make matters worse, no matter how hard I try to recall the rest of what happened, the memories are as sparse and scattered as leaves on an early autumn lawn. There's a gaping empty hole where memory should be, which makes me sick to my stomach."

"You had a blackout, which isn't uncommon for an alcoholic."

"That might be true, but it seems as if nothing's been going my way. My life feels empty. Miserable. Useless. Sometimes I wonder if I want to go on."

"That's the alcohol talking. With what you're telling me, I urge you to stop drinking immediately. The booze will only make you more vulnerable...less able to cope. I promise you, if you stop, I'll be there for you in anyway I can."

Ellie gave Maddie a weak smile, not convinced she had the strength or the motivation to put the 'plug in the jug.'

Back at her apartment after the meeting with Maddie, Ellie polished off the half-empty bottle of chardonnay, opened another and carried it into the living room. Time slipped by and she couldn't be certain how long she had been drinking and ruminating, when a knock on the door startled her. She quickly placed the bottle and glass in a side table and shut the drawer.

Another knock and a familiar voice rang out, "Are you in there? It's Damien. Let me in."

Ellie took a swig from a travel-sized bottle of mouthwash she kept in her purse, shuffled to the door and peered through the peep-hole. Damien stared back at her with a smirk on his handsome face. He had heard her, there was no turning back.

"Finally," he said when she opened the door.

"You're here early, why aren't you at work?" Ellie showed him to the sofa and took a seat next to him.

"I worked overtime yesterday so I took a couple hours off to be with my gal." He gave Ellie a hug and tried to kiss her, but she avoided his face so he wouldn't smell the alcohol on her breath."

"What's the problem?"

Being in a new relationship was like navigating an unstable sea. "Nothing to do with you. It's just that I've been having these flashes of memory about the night Jessica died."

"What kind of memory?"

"That I was in her apartment when the incident happened..."

"Now how can that be? You said you were home in your bed the next morning."

"I don't know. Maybe it's only a bad dream and nothing more, but it keeps recurring."

He sniffed the air. "Have you been drinking? I swear I smell something. Maybe the alcohol has caused these hallucinations."

Hallucinations? Was she having hallucinations? She couldn't be sure since there were so few puzzle pieces to put together and no coherent picture. "Perhaps you're right, it's all my vivid imagination. Nothing more."

"Yeah, I'm sure of it. Now, how about I get us something non-alcoholic to drink?" He rose and made his way into her tiny kitchen.

She watched him leave the room while admiring his long limbs, straight back, and the way his thick brown hair curled at the nape of his neck. Merely observing him from behind set off sparks. How lucky she had been to meet him at one of her first AA meetings.

She pictured herself standing alone, off to the side, too frightened to take a seat in the overcrowded, overheated room. And then he was there, by her side, introducing himself and leading her to a seat next to his. Even though newcomer relationships were discouraged in AA, they had been inseparable ever since. He was the salve to her grief over Jessica's death. She silently prayed she wouldn't ruin this relationship with her drinking, as she had with another one in the past. It was too precious a commodity to risk.

He returned with iced tea and handed her a glass. "Now lets talk about something more pleasant. I came over early to spend quality time with you. Let's make the most of it."

The next day at work, Ellie could barely function. Besides the booze secluded in her desk drawer, which she swigged on repeatedly, irritability and restlessness nagged at her. She could hardly concentrate on her assignments. When her boss came by to give her a new file with more paperwork to complete, she had trouble focusing on the data and filing the form. Since Juan Gonzales' immigration status hung solely on her doing her job as a paralegal, she had to finish the file before she left for the day.

She forced herself to shut out her jittery feelings and attend to the paperwork. Finally, file done and uploaded, she fished around under her desk, located her purse, and left a few minutes earlier than usual.

She had better start coping better or she would be out of a boyfriend...and a job. It was only a matter of time until she drank enough to ruin any opportunities life had presented to her in recovery. But what to do?

Hypnotherapy. She had researched it online this past weekend, hoping it might help her to recall more details about the night Jessica died. While numerous experts believed there wasn't much you could do to retrieve lost memory from a blackout, she had to try something before she lost her mind.

At her apartment, she poured a glass of wine, then opened her tablet and searched for hypnotherapists in the Queen Village area of Philadelphia. Although there was a sizable list, the first name on it was Sarah Abrams. Damien had mentioned that name to her a couple weeks back after Ellie first revealed she was thinking of seeing a therapist. The recommendation had come from Damien's AA sponsor, Hank. Dr. Abrams had successfully treated one of Hank's friends.

Ellie only hesitated for a couple of minutes. Then she picked up the phone and dialed Dr. Abrams' number.

Chapter Two

"And that's how Ellie came to be my patient," I tell a group of my colleagues clustered around a conference table during our weekly staff meeting to discuss our most interesting or formidable cases.

Aaron Davis, a fellow psychologist, in a gray suit and white shirt, scribbles notes on a legal pad, while two social workers, one beanstalk thin, the other decidedly more rotund, appear to hang onto my every word.

Meanwhile, Dr. Sam Roseburg, head of Psychiatry at the mental health clinic, gives me a nod of encouragement. "Tell us more about this patient, Sarah."

"Although I've only seen Ellie a total of three times, I'm already stymied by the complexity of her situation. Not only did she lose her closest friend recently, but since then, she's had recurrent, fragmented memories of the night her friend died, which are driving her batty...to use a professional term." Everyone laughs. "But what is challenging to me is the difficulty of helping her recapture memory during a blackout, even if it's only a fragmentary blackout, as it appears to be in this case."

"Fragmentary blackout," skinny social worker, Alice Meechan asks. "What's that?"

"There are actually two types of blackouts, en bloc blackouts and fragmentary blackouts. Fragmentary blackouts involve partial blocking of memory formation that occurred while the person was intoxicated, but they can ultimately regain limited memory of events, which means Ellie's situation isn't totally hopeless...at least I hope not."

Dr. Roseburg stands, grabs a cup of coffee off the side counter and rejoins us at the table. "Could you tell us more about what you've done in treatment so far?"

"To answer your question, I'd like to describe my first session with Ellie..."

"Ellie Ross?" I addressed a rather plain looking twenty-nine year old woman with tussled reddish brown hair and frightened hazel eyes who stared up at me from a seat in the waiting room. "Come this way."

Ellie stood, her shoulders hunched forward, making it difficult to judge her height, although she appeared to be on the tall side. The clothes on her slender frame fit her loosely and gave her the appearance of being slightly unkempt, as though she had hurriedly thrown herself together. All this led to my first impression of her as someone with little self-esteem.

She followed me into my office at the end of a long hall and took a seat across from me. "What can I do for you today?"

Ellie's eyes shifted nervously back and forth as they took in her surroundings. "I don't know if you can help me, but I don't know where else to turn?"

"Help you with what?"

She gnawed on a cuticle. "Since my best friend died less than two months ago, I've been having a hard time of it."

"In what way?"

Ellie proceeded to fill me in on the details of the death, her alcoholic blackout and the bits of what might be recovered memory, but also could be dream material, that has returned to haunt her.

I listened quietly while taking notes. "Since these 'memories' have only started to emerge over the past couple of weeks, what's changed in your life?"

She glanced down at her hands weaving invisible patterns in her lap. "I'm ashamed to admit this, but...but I drank again and, since then, my life has been turned upside down. It's like I'm losing everything I've worked so hard to find. And to top things off, these confusing flashbacks have been driving me bonkers.."

The distress in her voice alert me to the seriousness of her situation. I put aside my pen and pad and leaned toward her. "What would it take to make you stop drinking? What would have to occur?"

"I'd need to go back to my AA meetings."

"And how hard would that be for you?"

"Believe me, I'd love to do it, but I can't seem to make it happen..."

"What's preventing you?"

"Fear," she answered after a long hesitation. "And embarrassment. I mean, what will my AA friends think?'

"What will they think?"

She nibbed her nail again. "I don't know...most likely they'd be glad I'm back. They've been calling me, but I haven't answered the phone."

"And what does this have to do with your coming to see me?"

"I was hoping hypnotherapy might help me recall more about the night my friend died."

I hesitate, not wanting to give her false hope, but also reluctant to discourage her. "If we have any hope of coaxing those memories to the surface, you need to be clean and sober. Alcohol will only muddle your thinking and mask your feelings. I need you to make a commitment to toss away any alcohol you have on hand and go back to AA as soon as possible."

Ellie sighed. "Yeah, I know you're right. I need to do what you say."

"A commitment then? Will you commit to it?"

"Okay...yeah, I'll try–"

I interrupted her. "Try?"

"Okay, I'll do it."

"Good. I'd love to work with you, but I'd be wasting your time and money unless you're sober. I won't be able to begin hypnotherapy with you until you get back on the wagon. But when you do, I'll be more than happy to work with you and see what we can accomplish together..."

Cathy Clark, the pleasingly plump social worker, interrupts. "Good start..."

"And has it happened?" Aaron asks.

"According to her, she poured all the alcohol she had down the drain right after returning home from our session and went to a meeting the following night."

Sam Roseburg smiles supportively. "Good, because it's obvious we can do little to treat someone who is active in their addiction. I'm glad you insisted she return to AA. How many times have you seen her since she stopped drinking?"

"Twice, but I'm not doing her much good outside of getting her sober."

"That's a big deal," Sam says.

"I know, but I'm at a loss at how to help her retrieve more memories of that terrible night. I've tried using trance work both sessions, but it hasn't produce any real results. That's why I'm bringing this case to you."

"Hum...Do any of you know of a way to facilitate this work?" Sam asks.

Alice raises a hand. "From my experience, it can't be done." She glances over at her compadre Cathy and they exchange nods.

Sam turns to Aaron. "You've done a lot of work with addicts Aaron. Any ideas about this?"

"I'm afraid I won't be much help here either. I'll do my homework, but I don't know of any technique that has proven beneficial in this kind of case." He taps his pen against the tabletop. "I'd keep doing what you're doing for now and see if there's a breakthrough. If not, perhaps sodium pentothal, but I'm not sure how successful it will be with a blackout."

I glance at my notes, sensing the weight of Ellie's case. "Thanks, I appreciate all your guidance. I'm worried about Ellie. She's really struggling. Unless we make a breakthrough, I have to wonder if she'll be able to remain sober and functional."

Roseburg sips his coffee. "I admire your commitment to your client, Sarah, but we only have so much time to offer each person who comes through our doors. I'm sure you'll do whatever you can, but be aware, you can't do it indefinitely."

The frustration of working in a mental health system limited by medical insurance and administrators gnawed at me often in this new job. I loved working in private practice, but my brush with near death three and a half years ago had rendered working in an office alone at night untenable. And I have been worried sick since Drew's release from prison eight months earlier.

Drew. His name alone makes me tremble with apprehension. In spite of his confession to me, which he later denied, there wasn't enough evidence for the DA to charge him with anything greater than assault, which carried a maximum of five years. Fewer with good behavior. A murderer/rapist on the loose didn't exactly mollify my fears.

And now with him back on the street, trying to locate Rebecca, I'll be back in his cross-hairs. The thought sends chills scurrying along my spine. Drew's not only a calculating killer, he's a damn accomplished sociopath and manipulator. I doubt I have the smarts or the skill to outmaneuver him.

All that considered, it made sense to join the staff of a psychiatric facility and work in an institution with other professionals. Still, I can't help but question my decision at times like this. "I'll do what I can with the time I have left."

Sam glances at his watch. "Talk about time. I have to get to a meeting. Let's wrap it up for today."

Everyone rises and shuffles out of the room except me. I stay put at the table for a good five minutes longer trying to quiet my concern. Distraught at the idea of terminating a client in as much pain as Ellie Ross, I am damn well determined to figure a way out of this therapeutic impasse.

Chapter Three

Ellie

Back at her apartment after an evening session with Sarah, Ellie decided to tidy up before Damien made his appearance. Lately, he'd been arriving later and later, which was beginning to distress her more than she wanted to admit. She chided herself for her childish reaction. No one could be more loving than Damien. He couldn't help it if he had to work late. While he said he'd much rather be spending time with her and would apply for an earlier shift, nothing had become available so far. Why would she even consider making a problem out of this? She was blessed to have him in her life.

She opened her dresser drawer to place a pair of jeans away, when she noticed her pants weren't folded in her usual compulsively perfect pile. The sight of the disorderly pile troubled her more than she would have thought necessary, She squinted at the pants for a long moment trying to figure out if she had moved them aside when sorting through them that morning. Normally, she would have straightened them if she had.

She heard a knock, took a deep breath and closed the drawer quickly before plastering a stilted smile on her face in anticipation of greeting Damien.

"Hi Hon," he said on entering. He held out a bouquet of ruby red roses. "For you."

"How sweet of you." She inhaled the cloying scent of roses, then went into the kitchen, retrieved a vase and placed them in it, all the while feeling guilty for questioning his sincerity. "They're lovely."

"Just like you." He watched her set the vase on the coffee table, then bundled her into his strong arms. "I missed you like crazy today."

She hugged him back, bursting with elation at his attention and affection, which along with the roses, erased any doubts she had about him. Before she could kiss him, she detected the stench of burning food. "Oh no, smells like I'm scorching the casserole!" She took off for the kitchen and removed the overcooked enchilada casserole from the oven.

Damien withdrew a potholder from under the counter and placed it on the countertop for the casserole then took a seat at the dining room table. She scrapped the burnt cheese and browned sauce from the pan and served the dish. They dug into it, polishing off tortillas, chile and cheese in no time. Afterwards, they sipped on decafs while she inquired about his day and he asked about her therapy session.

She smiled to herself. Damien had taken quite an interest in her work with Sarah. While flattered by his concern, she knew it was at least partially motivated by his AA sponsor's curiosity. Hank had peppered Damien with questions about her therapy on a number of occasions since she started seeing Sarah. Since Hank had referred Ellie in the first place, she guessed there wasn't anything out of the ordinary about this.

After dinner they did the dishes together and watched The Daly Show snuggled up against one another on the sofa. Damien enclosed her in his arms and it didn't take long before the warmth of his touch, the soothing sexy scent of his cologne, eased all her earlier frets and fears. Any last remnants of distrust dissolved at the moment his lips touched hers.

Later, in the darkened bedroom, all her prior anxiety came rushing back at her. She crawled out of bed, not wanting to disturb Damien, and blind-touched her way into the living room, taking a seat on the sofa. Something was wrong and she couldn't deny it for long. Besides grieving Jessica and the loss of her sobriety, something more was plaguing her, something unnamed and unknown. She wasn't making much progress in therapy. Small matters, like the unkempt drawer, gnawed at her more than normal.

If only they could take a c-scan of her brain and see what was going on inside. Cut her open and peer into her neural pathways. But there was nothing they could do for her beyond hypnotherapy, and the fact that it wasn't working, had become unbearable. She wasn't certain what other avenues were open to her, but she would do anything in her power to recapture a more complete memory of her last night with Jessica.

Anything shy of drinking again.

Holding the hands of people on either side of her at the close of another meeting, Ellie recited the Serenity Prayer in concert with her AA group. A tall, dark, good-looking man to her right with tattoos on both arms and a black tee shirt that stretched across his muscular chest, reading, *Harley Hitman*, asked her if he could help put away her chair. Pleased with the offer, she accepted. He hung the folding chair on a rack and returned to gather his belongings.

"Thanks for helping me out."

"No problem," he said. "Any friend of Damien's is a friend of mine."

She studied him. He didn't look like anyone who impeccably groomed, stylishly dressed, professional Damien would hang around with, but you never knew in AA. "How do you know Damien?"

"I met him at a meeting a few weeks back and he asked me to sponsor him. I'm Hank."

She shook Hank's outstretched hand. "I'm so glad to meet you. Damien's mentioned you to me, but when did he mention me to you?"

Hank smiled. "Actually I was the one who pointed you out to him when you first arrived at that Saturday morning meeting because you looked so lost. It's always helpful for one alcoholic to reach out to another, but I wasn't expecting him to be quite as 'helpful' as he's become."

She laughed. "Oh, what terrible things has he told you about me?"

Hank grinned. "Only that he thought you were nice."

"Nice?" Not exactly what she wanted to hear, but better than nasty. Because of her doubts about Damien, what she really hoped to hear from Hank was how thrilled Damien was to be with her. Slightly letdown, she ignored her feelings in an attempt to make small talk with Hank and get to know him better, but all the while, she harbored a tiny, nagging sense of disappointment.

Chapter Four

"Ellie skipped her session last week and I immediately suspected a relapse, which, as you're well aware, is often the case with alcoholics or drug addicts who are non-compliant. But she appeared on time for her session earlier today looking rested and ready to do the work." I learn forward and place my elbows on the conference table. "She apologized for missing the session, but said it completely skipped her mind, which is usually a sign of growing resistance, not unusual at this point in the process. She told me she's attending AA meetings on a regular basis, meeting with her sponsor and beginning her step-work."

"Of course, that doesn't necessarily mean she didn't have a temporary set-back," Aaron points out.

"I realize that, but, if she did, it was short-lived. She couldn't have pulled herself together so quickly if she had a major relapse." Funny, I am a little put out by Aaron's remark. It's as though he's calling my observations into question. "She's hoping that starting her steps will help her to breakthrough her amnesia."

"Good luck with it," Aaron remarks with a roll of his eyes. "I've never heard of anyone reversing a blackout by doing their step-work. AA might be a good self-help program, but it's not miraculous."

Again, my gut twists. I don't know if what I'm sensing is a power play on Aaron's part, since he's the only other psychologist on the staff, or if I'm being protective of Ellie, but it's disquieting. While Aaron had been the first to befriend me when I took this job, lately he's been more dismissive of me. I'm not quite sure of the reason beyond professional rivalry.

"So," Sam pipes in, "did you attempt hypnotherapy again?"

"I tried a little something different this time, sand-tray work, to see if it would produce better results than I've had so far with the hypnosis?" I look around the table at all the blank stares. "It's a form of therapy that employs a sandbox and miniature objects." I pull out my cell phone and pass around a photograph of the finished sandbox. "I can better show you than describe it." I rise. "Would you mind following me into my office?"

Alice and Sally stand, but Aaron leans back in his seat. "I'm not sure what that will accomplish."

Challenged, I feel pressured to respond decisively. "It's better for me to demonstrate what happened during the session with Ellie instead of describing it. It shouldn't take more than a few minutes."

Sam starts toward the door and everyone joins him. Under pressure from the herd, Aaron sighs, rises and reluctantly trails behind. We all traipse down the hall to my office.

As soon as everyone is in my office, I say, "Take a seat and I'll try to recreate the session."

I wait until they're all seated and I position myself at the sand-tray a large box of sand on a side table surrounded by bookshelves of toys, small replicas of everyday objects and plastic people of both genders, all races, ages, and many vocations.

"I began the session by asking Ellie to recreate what she could remember about the night of Jessica's death by placing objects in the sand-box...

"Ellie studied the box for the longest time. 'I'm not sure what you want me to do.' She grabbed a plastic man in a suit then changed her mind. 'Or what this will do for me.'

I had dealt with resistance before when introducing the sand-tray. While it evoked a sense of play and lack of seriousness, the actual act of replicating a feeling or experience in the box made it more tangible and real, which could be incredibly anxiety provoking. I had learned when running headlong into this defensiveness the best way to get around it was to gently encourage my clients to experiment. 'Why don't you play with the tray for a few minutes and add only things you would enjoy having in your life.'

Ellie picked an iridescent blue glass ball off the shelf and placed it in the middle of the box. Next, she added a girl doll and surrounded her with a woman and a man who appreared to shield her from anything outside the box. Finally, she added a house to the side and drew a path in the sand to the front door. She turned and faced me with a triumphant smile. 'I did it.'

'You sure did. Can you tell me how it makes you feel?'

She moved the adults closer to the child. 'Wonderful. Looking at it makes me happy. The child seems safe. She has a home and she is loved.'

'Who is that child?'

'She's the child I want to have."

'Is that all?"

She hesitated. 'She's the child I always wanted to be. The loved child. The protected child.' A tear traveled down her cheek.

'How does she differ from you?'

Ellie wrapped her arms around herself. 'I never felt safe or loved with my parents. They were too busy working and taking care of my autistic brother. They never seemed to have enough time for me.' The single tear had multiplied into many. I handed Ellie a tissue.

'I always wanted to be an only child. Maybe then they'd have time for me. But that never happened and to this day, they're still fixated on my brother's well being and rarely have time for mine.'

I placed an arm around Ellie's shoulders and let her sob out the longing and sadness she still experienced over her family; the family that had left her with a hole in her soul she had tried for years to fill with alcohol.

Sam clears his throat. "I can see how effective this treatment can be, but were you able to get Ellie to recreate her experience the night of the murder?"

"Not this session, because of time restraint, but I plan to do it in the next."

"When do you plan to get back to the hypnotherapy?" Aaron asks, looking less than impressed.

"In time, but first let's see if this allows any unconscious memories to surface beyond her awareness. Working on a non-verbal level can permit her subconscious to sneak around those pesky defense mechanisms."

"Why not?" Alice agrees. "Its a great idea. I look forward to hearing about the next session."

Cathy shakes her head. "Me too."

Outnumbered, Aaron looks away.

"All right, then." Sam combs fingers through his thinning brown hair. He never appears as well dressed as Aaron Davis with his suits and ties. Sam is more the *Dockers* and *Izod* type, but even in his mid-fifties, he's trim and fit. "That's enough for today. Let's continue with this case next week after Aaron presents his latest and greatest."

Later the same day after my last session, I linger alone in my office going over my notes. Even after a busy afternoon, I still feel mildly irritated by the encounter with Aaron. Something's not working quite right between us and I can't figure out what it could be, which, as an analyst, annoys me no end. Perhaps I came on too strong with him, or he's threatened by how quickly I've risen in the ranks at the hospital. Although I can't see Sam Roseburg playing favorites, maybe Aaron can. I've been handed a couple of tough cases, similar to Ellie's. Maybe he believes it's because Sam trusts me more than him with these patients, but it's probably due to the fact that both are women in untenable situations...a specialty of mine.

Like one of my most memorable patients, Rachel Rosen. A prime example of this type of client, Rachel came to see me after being raped and having her husband murdered in the same incident. After months of hypnotherapy, Rachel successfully broke through a memory block to uncover the real criminal... the unforgettable Drew.

Even if Aaron experiences professional jealousy, real or imagined, there has to be a way to resolve our differences. We have been thrust together into a professional relationship and it would behoove us to overcome our differences and pull together as a team. I consider what has worked in the past in these types of situations, but nothing even close to this has ever presented itself before.

Then it comes to me. Why not collaborate more closely with him. If what he wants is more power and respect, wouldn't it be helpful to use him as a sounding board. The message would be clear: You are the professional whose opinion I admire. Hopefully, that would defuse any tension between us before it can evolve into all out warfare, a possibility I dread. Treating the dysfunctional and unstable can be draining enough without additional conflict within your support system.

I jot a note in Ellie's file and close it. Tomorrow I will experiment by approaching Aaron for assistance with this case. I can only pray my solution will work.

Chapter Five

Ellie

Upon entering her apartment after another exhausting day at the office, Ellie immediately went over to the refrigerator to pour herself a glass a wine. Then she remembered, no more wine for her, and she reached for bottled water instead. This recovery thing could be awfully trying at times. Thirsty, she gulped the water. She knew from past experience, the only real way to unwind after work without a drink was to take a walk. In the bedroom she changed into tights, a tee shirt and running shoes.

Outside the sun had dipped closer to the horizon, but it was still light enough to cover at least two miles before it disappeared. With all that was going on, she wanted to be back long before dark. Light or not, she hadn't gone more than a couple blocks before she had the sense of someone following her. She stopped. Looked around. Took a deep breath. Nothing she saw alarmed her.

Was she only being paranoid? A nervous wreck? She studied the playground across the street and watched to see if anyone exited the corner store before resuming her walk. Her pace had increased and she found herself covering more ground than she typically did. Again, she had the strange sensation of being followed. She turned around. Could she spot anyone? A woman across the street walked her dog and a couple of kids rode by on bikes. Otherwise, there were only a few suits scurrying home from work. Nothing out of the ordinary.

She had gone no more than another block before her skin began to crawl and Jessica's voice whispered; "Maddie, Maddie," in her ear. Shaken by what she heard, she covered her ears with her hands, wanting to silence the insistent voice.

Even if this was only her overactive imagination at work, it was defeating the purpose of her walk. Jumpier and more on-edge than she had been when she left her apartment, it was useless to continue this exercise in futility. She turned and scurried back in the direction of her apartment, certain she heard footsteps behind her, although when she turned no one followed. She fully expected to be snatched off the street every time she passed a high hedge or gate. By the time she reached her building, she couldn't catch her breath from full-blown panic. She rushed inside and slammed the front door.

No sooner had she locked the apartment door behind her, then she collapsed on the sofa, breathing rapidly. Heart racing. She didn't know for a fact that she had averted danger, but she certainly reacted as though she had. It took her more than fifteen minutes to calm herself enough to make dinner. Damien would be home shortly and she wanted to have dinner ready when he arrived. Besides, cooking would take her mind off her troubles.

At least she hoped it would.

Damien arrived home late, but not much later than usual. When he took her in his arms and gave her a big kiss, he seemed distracted and distant.

"You okay?" She asked when he drew back.

He offered her a weak and inauthentic looking smile. "Yeah, yeah...sure...I'm fine."

She studied him for a minute. "I don't believe you."

He stared at his shoes. "It's nothing for you to worry about. It's just that Oliver drank last night."

"Oh, no." Damien had sponsored Oliver for the last few weeks. At seventeen, Oliver had been like a son to him. She knew what this meant for Damien. Since he admired Oliver's motivation at such a young age, this had to hurt.

"I'm so sorry. I hate to picture Oliver that way."

Damien looked stricken. "I went by his house before heading home. He's as smashed as a two car collision. He can hardly walk without stumbling and he's slurring his words. It's horrible."

At the memory of her recent relapse, guilt cramped her stomach. "I'm sure it is."

Damien lowered himself onto the sofa. "I can't believe this is happening. He seemed so committed. How can it be?"

She took the seat beside him and snaked an arm around his shoulders. "Are you tired? You look it."

Damien lowered his head to his hands, looking terribly defeated. "Exhausted. This emotional stuff takes it out of you."

"Yeah, I know. I'm so sorry you have to deal with this, but don't give up hope. He might still return. I did."

He patted her hand. "I'm so glad to hear you voicing a commitment to your recovery. I've been concerned about you, too, at times."

Again her gut twisted with shame, knowing her commitment hadn't always been strong or sincere. Would she be able to live up to his expectations...and hers? She wanted to with all her heart and she wasn't typically a quitter when she set her mind to a goal, but this recovery stuff was different. She looked at him and a warmth spread through her. "If I can't do it for myself, can I do it for you?"

He squeezed her hand. "Do it for anyone you can."

She only prayed she could.

Later, as Ellie prepared for bed, she went to her lingerie drawer for her nightgown. When she opened the drawer, she had the odd sense something was amiss. While she had placed her cotton gown on top of the pile of nightwear, it was now under two other nighties. Strange. This was the second time her drawers had been breached and it confirmed the first.

She extracted the gown, but even touching it gave her the creeps. Had a stranger been fingering her nighty? A wave of revolution poured through her. She dropped the nightgown into her laundry basket and picked out another for the night.

Was her sense of her intrusion well founded, or was she simply "hallucinating," as Damien had suggested? She had a strong suspicion someone was on her tail. But who was it and how were they getting into her apartment? And if it were true, why were they being so elusive that all she had to go on were her feelings and a few misplaced items of clothing? She was beginning to believe she might be going crazy. That all she believed, and all she experienced, were merely figments of her imagination. Perhaps she had been drinking long and hard enough to have done real damage to her central nervous system. All that was possible.

Her impulse was to share what she was going though with Damien and use him as a point of reference, but he had been so upset all evening about Oliver's relapse, she didn't want to burden him. Perhaps she would be able to tell him at another time. In the meantime, she was left to struggle with these fears and uncertainties on her own. If someone had invaded her space, she might be in grave physical danger. But, if her suspicions were only a result of alcohol organicity, she might be in danger of losing her mind. She wasn't certain which was worse.

Either way, she was screwed. The only difference—either someone was screwing with her or she was screwing herself. And, until she knew the truth, she had better be vigilant and self protective. That is, if she could against such an illusory enemy.

Chapter Six

Sarah

Alice Meechan gazes at me with an expectant expression. "So, what happened in your next session with Ellie?"

Since I didn't want to make everyone take the long walk to my office a second time, I had sketched a roughly drawn printout of her sand-tray work. I hand the drawings around the table. When I give him one, Aaron smirks at me.

"My 6 year old could do better than this."

"I'm sure she could, but this is not meant as a professional drawing. It's only instructive, not artistic." I don't want to repeat the tense interaction with Aaron another time, so I keep my voice soft to defuse the conflict. "As you can see, I followed up the previous session with Ellie by asking her to create a sand-tray of the night Jessica was murdered."

"What is this?" Sam asks, pointing out a miniature table in the middle of the sand-tray surrounded on one side by black buttons made to look like stools.

"That's Ellie's rendition of a sleazy bar. Complete, you will notice, with bottles lined on shelving behind it," I explained. "And over here is the living room at her friend's apartment," I point to a separate area of the tray. "There is a sofa, chair and coffee table."

"And this, I assume, is the bedroom." Aaron sniggers. "What does this show that you don't already know."

"Not much yet. When creating the tray, she described exactly the same thing she had told me before, but when I asked her to show me what had happened at the apartment, she floundered." I steeped my fingers and lowered by chin to them. "That's as far as we've gotten."

Aaron smirks. "So you're stuck."

Given the opportunity to change the timbre of my relationship with him, I ask, "Do you have any idea what might help me out?"

"Terminate this case. No use wasting anymore of your time and offering her false hope."

The exact reaction I hoped to avoid. "But I haven't even tried all the tools in my box yet. I can't see sending her on her way until I've done everything possible."

"Yeah, good luck." Aaron grunts. And my stomach twists in a knot.

As I wander back to my office after the staff meeting, the receptionist, Janice, stops me as I pass her desk.

"How come you warrant a window cleaning when no one else gets the same VIP treatment?"

Surprised, I freeze. No one informed me about a window cleaning. Had someone been in my office while I was out? "My windows weren't supposed to be cleaned today. Are you sure about that?"

"All I know is that a guy came by with all the equipment...not a bad looking guy either...and told me Roseburg had arranged to have your windows cleaned. Should I not have let him into your office?"

I flex my brow. "I would think that Roseburg would have informed me about the cleaning so I could schedule my appointments." It might be spring, but I'm suddenly chilled. Who could have been in my office? Could it possibly be Drew back for more? Was he trying to locate information on my former client, Rachel? Thank goodness I had locked my file cabinet before I left for the meeting. "Next time don't let anyone in unless I give you a heads up ahead of time. Okay?"

"Sure...sure. I'm sorry about that. I had no idea."

"I know," I said. "But now you do."

As soon as I enter the office, I sense the intrusion. Perhaps it is simply because I know someone has been in the office because nothing is obviously out of place. I sniff the air and suddenly a faint, but familar scent fills my nostrils, along with a sense of dread. I open the top drawer and notice the notepad has moved. While it could have shifted when I opened the drawer, I'm pretty certain of who and what I am dealing with here, and I don't like it one bit. I'm not keen on having a sick psychopath like Drew on my tail again. The police detective at central station said I could call at any time and they would be right over.

This might be the time to make that call.

Later, when I leave the building, I scan the parking lot in every direction before making my way to my car. I quickly drive out of the lot and straight to my sister's house in Lower Merion. Not wanting to worry her, I try my best to quiet my anxiety on the way over. The last thing I want to do is remind her of all we'd been through with Drew's trial and conviction. She stood by my side the entire time and, for that, I am immensely grateful, but I don't want to put her through the ordeal again.

Lara opens the door looking as radiant as ever in her blue satin shirt and tailored jeans. She has managed to corner all the beauty in the family, but because of her wonderful nature, I am rarely ever jealous or resentful. Even though I am decidedly plainer than her, her beauty lights me from within. I adore being in the glow of her love.

She gives me one of her big, generous hugs, but then pushes me away and studies me. "Okay, what is it?"

Damn. I always wear my heart on my face and in the way I carry myself. No use fooling her. "Drew was released from prison. He's out on parole."

Lara's smile fades fast. She turns pale. "Already?"

"Good behavior, I guess."

She leads me to the living room sofa. "What can we do?"

"Nothing just yet. Let's see what he does."

"Shit!"

I rarely hear Lara swear so I take notice. "Don't worry, I'm doing what I can to protect myself. I have the stun gun you gave me, I've notified the police, the hospital has been informed and I'll be extremely cautious no matter where I'm going or what I'm doing."

"That doesn't exactly reassure me," Lara says through clenched teeth. "How about moving in with me for a time?"

Although expected, not exactly what I want. "I can't put you and your family at risk. There's no way I would do that."

"You are stubborn, Sarah. You can't stay at your townhouse alone. You're too vulnerable."

Of course, she's right. I might as well place a bullseye on my forehead. Living by myself, I'm an easy target. "I'll figure something out. Perhaps I can talk my friend Scott into moving in with me for awhile. Having a man around might scare Drew away."

Lara shakes her lovely head. "From what I know of Drew, nothing will scare him away if he thinks you have what he wants. I'm petrified for you."

"Don't worry, I'll figure this out." I'm petrified, too...but what else can I do?

Chapter Seven

Ellie

Ellie dreaded meeting with Jack after work on Thursday to discuss a memorial for Jessica. For some unexplained reason—at least to her satisfaction–he had repeatedly put her off. It had taken weeks to pin him down to a time and place, and when she finally did, he had insisted on getting together at a bar, where he would expect her to drink with him. Hard enough staying sober on her own, she didn't need the pressure her old drinking buddy would most certainly apply. While this was supposed to be happy hour, it was a profoundly unhappy for her.

She entered Sasha's to the beat of the Rolling Stones. This was an older crowd, not the Beastie Boys set. A strobe light flashed in her eyes as she wandered past the dance floor to the oak and glass bar. Jack jumped off his barstool to greet her. He looked a little rough about the edges for a thirty-five year old man, but that's what too much *Jägermeister* and late nights on the town will do for you. A day-old beard speckled his jaw and his complexion was sallow.

He gave her a squeeze, then stood back. "My, oh my, Miss Ellie, you sure looks fine tonight."

She laughed at his southern twang. "Y'all don't look so piqued yourself, Mr. Jack."

With a ceremonial sweep of his arm, he indicated an empty barstool next to his. "Please have a seat my fine lady."

He gestured at the bartender to order her a drink, but she stopped him before he could call her over. "I'm not drinking, Jack."

He cocked his head and raised a woolly brow. "My, my, my, Miss Ellie, you are full of surprises this evening."

"Don't let my abstinence ruin your drinking."

He smiled, a reptilian smile, "You don't have to worry your little head about that, darlin'," and downed the tall glass in front of him, before ordering another *Jägermeister* for himself and a Shirley Temple for her.

"Why the Shirley Temple?" she asked as soon as they were again alone. "I usually like a club soda with lime."

"This is a festive evening. Let's not ruin it with the mundane."

The last thing she would label this evening was festive. She had agreed to meet with Jack to discuss the memorial. Besides the drinking, why was Jack in such a buoyant mood? "Aren't we here to talk about Jessica's memorial?"

Jack's expression mutated from radiant to sullen as quickly as a chameleon caught in an unexpected spot. "Of course we are. I'm trying to lighten the mood a bit. I know Jessica would be having the time of her life if she could join us."

"Perhaps, but Jessica can't join us...she's dead."

His affect changed. "What a party pooper you are, Ellie. What would Jessica think?"

"I don't know about Jessica and I can't ask her, but I'm not exactly in a celebratory mood."

The bartender placed the drinks in front of them. Jack took a gulp from his. "You sure you don't want a real drink?"

"No I'm okay."

"Well, I'm not. This thing with Jessica is eating me alive. You know what Jessica meant to me."

Actually, she hadn't thought about the fling between Jack and Jessica for a long time. Not since Jessica told him she only wanted to be friends. Ellie had dismissed this as a passing phase, not as a more permanent condition. Listening to Jack now, she realized it hadn't been fleeting for him at all. He'd been more serious about Jessica than she realized. "Were you still in love with her?"

Jack stared at his drink as though the bubbles might lift his mood. "I will always be in love with her. I was heartbroken when she broke it off, but I have forgiven her."

"How long did you two see one another?"

Jack looked away. "On and off for years, my dear."

"I never knew..."

"It began years before you came into the picture. I figured Jessica must have told you, but by the time you joined our merry revelers, it was coming to an end...at least that's what Jessica wanted. I never relinquished the idea she might change her mind."

A strange sensation settled in Ellie's stomach and, as she habitually did, she took a sip of the Shirley Temple hoping to quiet it. Why did this new information disturb her? Did it have anything to do with her flashbacks?

Jack had lowered his head into his hands. Ellie placed a hand on his shoulder to comfort him. "This must be incredibly difficult for you."

When Jack raised his head, there were tears in his eyes. "You can't imagine."

He was right...she couldn't quite make sense of his reaction...or hers. "Lets talk about what we can do to honor our mutual friend."

He downed his drink and ordered another. "Okay, but first I want you to keep what I told you under wraps."

She involuntarily lowered her drink to the bar top with so much force it made a knocking sound. Jack twitched in response. "Why? What does that have to do with anything?"

"Because I'd like to keep it between us. I don't want the police snooping into my affairs anymore than they already have. If they catch wind of what I feel for Jessica, I might be under suspicion, which is ridiculous since Jessica was my best friend. I loved her too much to ever harm her. There's no reason to kick up dust in this investigation, especially dust that's already settled and forgotten."

Ellie sat back, perplexed. Jack's tone was strident. His words adamant. He leaned in a bit too close for her comfort. While she hadn't originally thought Jack had anything to do with Jessica's death, she now questioned her assumption.

He might not be under police suspicion, but he had triggered hers.

An hour later, Jack left the bar in a hurry, after glancing at his watch and saying he was late for a date. They had divvied up the responsibilities for arranging the memorial. She would secure the venue, Jack would contact the guests. They would meet again when they were ready to finalize their plans.

Ellie sat back and nursed her second Shirley Temple, Jack's revelation still playing a tune in her head. Not only was she surprised by his insistence on secrecy, but by how little she understood about Jack...or Jessica. Funny, these are the people she thought she knew best. But what did she really know about them?

The bartender stopped by and asked if she wanted a refill. They bantered back and forth for a minute, commenting on the weather and the crowd that evening. Then he grabbed her glass. "Another highball?" he asked.

She opened her mouth to correct him, but before she had a chance he moved on. She considered signaling him, but for an unknown reason, she didn't. She sat still, contemplating the idea of the highball and, suddenly, it sounded right. By the time he returned with it, she was ready for a drink.

She lifted the glass to her lips, sucked it down and experienced the instantaneous, giddy sensation of mild intoxication. While a sense of guilt nagged at her, the sedative effect of the drink quickly soothed her nerves and put her at ease. She loved this shit. No doubt about it.

After her forth drink she finally pulled herself away from the bar. It was late and Damien might be home. She didn't want to appear drunk or she'd never hear the end of it. Better to curve her consumption...for now.

She skipped the few blocks back to the apartment in a state of elation, invigorated by the alcohol. She reveled in it.

Luckily Damien had left a message that he would be home late and she had an hour before he arrived to eat a sandwich and sober herself up enough to face him. An hour and a half later he showed up, looking more exhausted than usual. Immediately after entering the apartment, he collapsed on the sofa, never noticing her condition. She couldn't believe her relief.

In the middle of the night, Ellie was startled awake in the living room of Jessica's apartment by a loud, metallic sound. Leveraging herself up with an elbow on the arm of the overstuffed side chair, she peered into Jessica's bedroom. What was going on in there? All she could see was a man standing by the bed with his back to her. She craned her neck and took note of the brown cordovan loafers, the navy and white pinstriped shirt and khaki chinos pants. She could barely make out a silver ring with a large blue stone on his dangling arm. When he pivoted in her direction, she quickly lowered her head against the back of the chair and closed her eyes so he wouldn't know she was awake.

Jessica voice filled her head; 'Ellie, Ellie.' She had the urge to react, but footsteps coming in her direction frightened her enough that she squeezed her eyes shut. When the footfalls retreated, she tried to rise, but was paralyzed, unable to move. The more she struggled, the more incapacitated she became...

She awoke in the midst of a full-blown panic attack, short of breath, with sweat beading her forehead and dribbling onto her pillow.

Too hysterical to fall back to sleep, Ellie sat up in bed, retrieved a pad and pen from the night stand and documented everything she could remember about the dream. Such an odd dream, it had seemed so real. She questioned how much of the dream corresponded with what she knew about that night. When the man turned toward her, why had she pretended to be asleep? Was she afraid of something?

It had been such a long time since she had a flash of memory, she could hardly wait for her mid-day session with Sarah. And, while it wasn't entirely clear that this memory was authentic, it was the closest thing she had to a breakthrough in weeks. Hopeful she might still be able to piece the puzzle together, she was also cautious. This could all be a red herring and have nothing to do with reality. A nightmare. Smoke and mirrors.

She could only pray that her dreams were leading her somewhere and weren't a subconscious attempt to obfuscate the facts.

She awoke the next morning with a familiar hangover and was immediately reminded of the one she had the morning after Jessica's death. Hangovers were hard to forget, but even in that context, her hangover on that particular morning was one heck of a doozy.

She had opened her eyes to searing light, the snow-refracted morning sunlight that illuminated her bedroom as it snaked its way through the cracks in the blinds and glared into her retinas. Her mouth had been unbearably dessicated and, when she reached for the water glass to take a desperate sip, she almost knocked it off the side table. Rising ever so slowly, her head throbbed and her limbs ached. She could barely lift her body off the bed.

Along with the obvious physical manifestations, came the more subtle, but no less painful, emotional ones. The flush of panic always appeared first. The question of what she had done the night before and who she had done it with, followed by a deep-seated certainty that whatever she did was nothing to be repeated, and whoever she did it with was no one she would ever want to see again. The acid burn of guilt for losing control over herself was followed by a strong desire to call Jessica and find out what horrendously embarrassing things she had said and done. Only later did the sinking feeling of despair and self-deprecation take over and nudge out the fear.

She stumbled over to the sink, splashed cold water on her face, cupped her hands to take a mouthful. She scrubbed her teeth to brush away the slime that clung to them as well as the coating on her gums. After forcing a brush through tangled hair, she looked in the mirror, her complexion paler than usual, her hazel eyes bloodshot. Even her curly, auburn hair, looks faded and limp. No erasing the damage she had done with soap or shampoo.

To ease the nausea in her gut, Ellie took a chug of Milk of Magnesia and washed it down with a glass of water, but it caused her to choke on the chalky taste and upchuck the entire solution. After downing a couple more glasses of water to rehydrate and mitigate her relentlessly arid mouth, she finally felt well enough for a cup of coffee.

But one sip of the rich brewed Columbian and she was back in the bathroom throwing up. She crawled back into bed. I never, ever, ever want to do this to myself again. She had promised herself she wouldn't do it so many times, but she never seemed to keep her promise. Maybe this time would be different. Maybe after being sick, she would be motivated enough to stop. But was she only fooling herself? Why would this drunk be any different than the scores of drunks before?

The phone rang. Fully expecting it to be Jessica, she answered on the third ring. "How are you doing this morning?"

To her surprise, Jack answered. "I'm okay, but I have bad news for you."

She gripped the phone closer. "What's going on?"

"You haven't heard?"

"Heard what? Explain yourself, man."

"You better take a seat." Jack cleared his throat. "They found Jessica this morning. Dead. According to what I've heard, she fell and hit her head on the metal file cabinet in her room. Sliced it open. They said she died quickly."

Ellie had heard what Jack was saying, but it seemed to be coming from a far away place, his voice hazy, as though he was speaking through a distortion device. Nothing he told her made any sense. "That's not funny, Jack."

"I know. This isn't one of my jokes."

The phone had slid out of her hand and hung from its chord off the nightstand. She grasped herself, doubled over off the side of the bed and dry-heaved her shock and misery into the waste paper basket. From a distance she heard Jack calling her name, asking if she was all right. When she could, she lifted the receiver. "I can't talk now," she said through sobs. "I'll call you later."

Before he had a chance to say anything else, she disconnected. She had been with Jessica in the bar only minutes or hours before she died. She wanted desperately to remember what they had been doing, but all she could recall was the vodka martini. What had happened after that was anyone's guess. Not only did the miasma of stale alcohol and mental confusion hang over her, it was as if a giant eraser had eliminated all recall. She didn't know how she had traveled from the bar to bed, or what had transpired in between, but she knew the next phone call would be from the police and they would expect details. She wanted to be helpful, but what could she tell them?

The phone rang and her throat constricted. She might have been the last person to see Jessica alive, and yet she had no recollection of anything that might be useful. She doubled over again in despair.

Chapter Eight

"Ellie told me about her dream...or would you call it a nightmare...in as much detail as she could recall. It was as vivid and descriptive as anything she had ever reported to me," I tell the group.

Aaron leans back in his chair, picking at an errant nail. He seems totally disinterested. I'm surprised when he asks, "Are you saying she had a relapse the night before having this dream?"

"That's right, but I'm not sure what the relapse has to do with anything. What's essential here is that she may have recalled in detail what occurred the night her friend died."

"Maybe so," Aaron replies. "But it's interesting to me that this is the second time one of these 'flashbacks' came during a relapse. There might be a pattern."

Aaron might be onto something. Ellie had been drinking the first time she recalled the fight in Jessica's apartment. "That's a really good point. I'm glad you mentioned it."

Sam clears his throat. "I don't give a hoot if there's a pattern, I hope you dealt with her relapse, memory or not."

Not surprising that Sam would be more concerned with her drinking than her revelation. "Naturally, I made sure she reported her relapse to her sponsor and went to an AA meeting that evening. I checked on her the next day and she had followed through on my recommendations. She was terribly ashamed of her behavior, and appalled by how easily her disease had slipped past her safeguards and insinuated itself back into her life. This episode stunned her into sobriety. It made her reconsider her commitment to staying clean and sober, which isn't a bad thing, after all."

Sam looks pleased and shakes his head in agreement. "Relapse can be useful at times. It can shock an addict into admitting their powerlessness and act as an impetus to get them to adhere to a recovery program. And, the fact that this relapse was so short and sweet is particularly hopeful for Ellie's recovery. It sounds like you did a good job."

Although I'm flattered by Sam's praise, I don't want to overestimate my role in Ellie's decision. "I guess you could attribute a small part of Ellie's recovery to the fact we're forming a strong therapeutic bond, but it has more to do with her commitment to herself than her commitment to me. I believe her when she tells me she's determined to be sober and to live her life differently. Jessica's death sealed the deal on Ellie's desire to stop drinking and 'get a life', as they say."

"Personal motivation is always more powerful than doing it for somebody else, or even for the Court or a job," Sam tells the group. "You're doing fine work, Sarah, but it's reassuring to know that Ellie has a personal commitment to sobriety."

The two social workers nod in agreement.

Aaron stops picking his nail. His gaze settles on me. I have the distinct sense he's gearing up to pick a fight. "How do you explain Ellie's lack of commitment to sobriety the night before your session? From what you've told us, she slipped so easily, without even the slightest shove."

On the spot, I can sense my hands tremble, so I place my water glass on the table. "I...I don't know how to explain it, although I often hear these stories from addicts. It's as though a part of their unconscious refuses to accept the fact they can't drink or use. Whatever the trigger, that part gains an upper hand in certain vulnerable situations. As an addictions expert, I'm sure you know what I mean."

"It might look unmotivated and spontaneous, but there must be some logical underlying reason for the relapse. I have trouble believing it's merely an unconscious event and that she didn't choose to drink. I believe she's using that as an excuse." Aaron has steel in his eyes.

I don't want to be forced to defend an indefensible position. "You might be right, but I can only report what she told me happened in the way it did. I know one thing, the entire incident shook her to the core and made her look more closely at herself. That's not saying she won't have another relapse, but it is saying that for now, it's renewed her determination to remain sober and face herself and her problems without the use of alcohol to buffer her feelings." Relieved when Aaron slumps back in his seat, but dry in the mouth at the close confrontation, I take another sip of water. "As you know, any drug will anesthetize emotions and blunt our ability to deal with life on life's terms. And that goes on long after an alcoholic sobers up. The long term damage done to the central nervous system doesn't immediately heal. It can take months, or even years, before they are truly able to experience their emotions in a constructive way again."

"Actually," Sam chimes in, "the way a drug like alcohol works is to stimulate the production of brain chemicals that numb emotion. Over time the alcohol depletes the neuron-transmitters in the central nervous system that protect us from our own reactions to situations. Once the alcohol is withdrawn, feelings are allowed to pour back into the brain like water through a broken dam because there's not much left to blunt their impact. The alcoholic is not only overwhelmed, but they have no way of identifying these foreign feelings, or anyway to cope with them. It takes time for recovering addicts to begin to recognize their emotions and compartmentalize them in a way that makes them manageable. And it takes time for the brain to heal to the point where it can produce enough neuro-chemicals to counteract and soften the onslaught of emotions. That's in part why newcomers in recovery are more apt to relapse. This may help explain Ellie's seemingly mindless slip."

I am relieved at Sam's explanation. It counteracts Aaron's rather cynical and argumentative viewpoint. "I'm afraid I have a session with Ellie in a few minutes and need a bit of time to go over my notes." I rise. "Thank you all for your participation in this case study today. I appreciate your help."

As I exit the room, I notice the expression on Aaron's face. While I might have won this battle, the war has yet to be decided.

I take a few minutes to center myself before leaving my office to seek Ellie in the waiting room. She sits to the side, reading a copy of *Vogue.* I observe her as I approach. Her mass of curly reddish brown hair formed spirals around her pale face and partially obscures her bloodshot hazel eyes. While thin, she is also lanky and long limbed. Since I'm not exactly known for my striking beauty, I am reticent to judge Ellie, but I have to admit neither of us can totally rely on our looks. In a culture that puts so much emphasis on appearance, we are slightly handicapped and have to compensate with our other attributes. It's interesting that Ellie has found someone so easily. The only thing I can attribute that to is AA.

Ellie spots me and rises abruptly, knocking the magazine to the floor. She retrieves it awkwardly and places it back on the pile.

I ignore her clumsiness. "How are you?" I ask as we leave the waiting area, walking side by side down the corridor.

"All right," she answers.

I am about to question her further when I turn the corner and accidentally bump into Aaron, who's standing in the middle of the hall talking on the phone with his back to me. "Excuse me."

Aaron, who half-turns clutching the phone to his chest, is about to say something to me, when he looks past me and his expression changes to wonder.

"Ellinor, how nice to see you."

"Hi Aaron," Ellie says to him. "Long time no see. How are you?"

Surprised, I look from one to the other. "You two know each other?" I ask, wondering why Aaron never mentioned this before.

Aaron smiles. "Ellie and I go back a long way. I used to date a friend of hers."

Ellie's smile fades. "Haven't you heard? Jessica died over two months ago."

Aaron gasps. "Your kidding me. Jessica. Dead. What happened?"

I hold up a hand. Since I never mentioned Jessica's name in the staff meeting and Aaron obviously hadn't put Ellinor together with Ellie, I want to protect our professional communication and not make Ellie uncomfortable. "This is not the time or place to discuss things of this nature." I cock my head toward a couple of other staff members chatting in the hallway. "I'm sure Ellie can tell you more about it at another time."

Aaron frowns. "Okay, you're right, but I want to know. I still have your cell number. Would it be okay if I call you?"

Ellie shrugs. "Sure. Anytime."

My gut twists. Something is not right here. "Ellie and I have a session now, but I'll speak with you later."

I hustle Ellie into my office and away from any possible professional conflict. Once seated, I ask, "Was Jessica the friend that Aaron dated?"

Ellie's expression turns somber. "Not only dated. He was in love with her, like every other man I knew."

"And how long ago was this?"

"Well over a year now. Jessica went out with him for a few months, but then he began to get on her nerves. She dumped him like a pan of dirty dishwater, but he refused to accept it. For months afterwards, he would come around and ask me about her. It broke his heart."

"I'm sorry for that." But even sorrier to think Aaron, contrary to what he had said, might have known my patient's identity all along. This could explain his defensiveness and hostility when discussing the case. Was he trying to throw me off-course? Protect himself? Was his behavior at seeing Ellie simply an act? And why?

While Ellie and I went on to talk about her week, and she told me in detail about all the meetings she had attended and what she had done to cement her sobriety, my mind kept slip-sliding back to Arron. The chance meeting had presented more questions than answers.

Questions only Ellie could answer. If only she could recover the truth.

Chapter Nine

Ellie

A week after their prior meeting, Jack left a message asking Ellie to meet him at the Irish Pub on 12th Street to go over the final guest list and other details for the memorial, scheduled in just over two weeks. Reluctant, after her misadventure the last time she met with Jack, she agreed to the arrangement, but set a definite time limit to their encounter. She told him she would have to be home by seven to cook dinner and he concurred.

She arrived at the pub with its early 19th Century ambiance and took a seat at the long rosewood bar. Behind the bar the rosewood shelving contained recessed lighting and stain glass panels. Jack had yet to arrive, but she ordered a club soda with lime to minimize the possibility of his offering to buy her a drink. He showed up a few minutes after the bartender placed the glass in front of her.

After hoisting himself onto a barstool, he cased the room for other women. "How're you doing?" He asked, his attention elsewhere.

"Fair to middling. You?"

Obviously failing to find what he was searching for, Jack turned back to her. "I've been better." He signaled the bartender and ordered a scotch and soda. She hadn't remembered him ordering that before. Jack's taste in liquor had definitely improved. "What have you been doing?"

"Nothing out of the ordinary," and they continuing bantering until his drink arrived. She sipped on her soda while he gulped down his scotch and ordered another.

"These drinks are lame. They should put some alcohol in 'em," he quipped, smiling.

She smiled back, but her heart wasn't in it. "So, you wanted to go over the list of Jessica's friends to invite to the memorial." She extracted a paper from her purse and handed it to him. "That should cover most of them."

He looked it over. "Where's Jim Evans' name?"

"Who the heck is Jim Evans'?"

"The guy she was dating when she died. You must have known about him."

No, she didn't. Jessica had never mentioned that she was seeing anyone on a steady basis. "What can you tell me?"

"She met him at the gym. Nothing too special about him, if you ask me."

"How do you know so much about him? I was Jessica's BFF and I didn't know a thing."

"Jessica mentioned it to me."

"Why don't I believe you?" Ellie asked, although it was a rhetorical question. She knew why she didn't believe him because it didn't compute. Why would Jessica tell him about this guy and not mention anything to her. It didn't make sense. "Were you tailing Jessica?"

He flushed crimson. "What do you mean? Why would I do such a thing?"

"Because you were still in love with her. Were you following her?"

He stood abruptly, rattling the barstool and almost knocking over her drink. "What the hell are you accusing me of? I'm not a stalker?"

"I don't believe Jessica would reveal something to you if she was keeping it from me."

He sneered. "Maybe Jessica wasn't as good a friend as you wanted to believe."

It took a full minute for Ellie to process what he was implying. Could it be true that Jessica had purposefully left her out of the conversation? And why would she do that?

"I still don't believe you. From your reaction, you were doing something that makes you uncomfortable."

He took a last slug of his scotch and waved the paper at her. "I have all I need to do an *evite*. I'll talk to you later."

He turned on his heels and marched out the door. She watched, still stunned by his reaction to her question. Could there be more to this than she knew, and what could that be? She hoped with his attitude she could find out or she'd never put this thing to rest.

Ellie left the bar after paying the tab, dragged herself home and immediately collapsed on the sofa. Before long she had descended into a deep sleep. By the time she awoke, it was close to eight. Damien was due to stop by at 8:30 and she hadn't even begun to prepare dinner. She forced herself to rise from her resting place and trudged into the kitchen, where she placed a pot of water on the stove to boil for whole wheat pasta with pesto. Thank goodness for *Trader Joe's* when in a rush.

Dinner done, Ellie took a seat on the sofa and turned on cable news. She watched a half-hour of *CNN* and then checked on the cold food. It would only take a moment to reheat, but it was never the same the second time around. Exasperated Damien had failed to call, to let her know he'd be late, and tell her when he expected to arrive, she grasped her cell off the coffee table and dialed his number. The phone immediately went to voicemail.

After leaving a message, she sat back and waited for the return call. Another half an hour more of cable news was all she could stand. Her stomach growled and she could no longer wait for dinner. She helped herself to a heaping bowl of pasta and reclaimed her sofa seat. Damn, she was frustrated. She knew Damien worked the late shift, but she didn't expect him to be this late. Why hadn't he called her? Wasn't that common courtesy? And where was he at this late hour?

At times like this it seemed as if she was struggling to stay afloat, and there was no one around to toss her a life jacket. While this was her life story, maybe it was also the human condition. Maybe we all struggled to keep our heads above water to one degree or another, and our search for a significant person, a relationship, an answer to our problems, was only an illusion, because no one can save us from ourselves. Ultimately, existentially, when confronted by tough times, we were always on our own. But even if that were true, it didn't make her feel any less distressed about Damien's absence.

She placed her empty bowl in the sink and changed the channel to a BBC mystery on PBS. Resting her head against a sofa pillow, her eyelids began to droop.

The sound of the door opening jerked her awake. With racing heart, she shot upright. Damien entered the apartment.

"Sorry I'm late. It was a long day."

Half asleep, she rubbed her eyes. "How'd you get in?"

He held up a key. "I knocked, but you must have been asleep so I used your spare key. I'll put it back."

"Don't bother. Hold onto it in case this happens again."

"Thanks."

She glanced at her watch. 9:35. "Where the hell have you been?"

His expression turned sour. "Why the interrogation? The boss needed me to go over some accounting."

"And you were nowhere near a phone?"

He looked even more annoyed, but so was she. "I was busy. I didn't have time to call. I wanted to get done and get out of there."

Usually she went out of her way to accommodate him, but not this time. She knew he was a catch and she was lucky to have him, but she was growing tired of being his doormat. "A two minutes phone call would not be a deal breaker, but not letting me know what's going on is. I bothered to make you one of your favorite dinners and it's sitting in the kitchen with frost forming on top. I can't be doing this anymore. If you plan to be late you need to let me know or I don't want you to come by at all. From now on, I'm putting dinner in the freezer if I don't hear from you in a reasonable amount of time."

He stepped back with an angry expression, but as soon as he saw the fire in her eyes, it softened to chagrin. She had never had the nerve to confront him so bluntly before, but this disappearing/reappearing act had driven her to the brink. Her fury had overridden her usual timidity and restraint in these matters.

"I'm so sorry, babes. I didn't know how much I was putting you out. I would never want to do anything to upset you."

He took the seat next to her on the sofa. "I made a mistake. Can you forgive me?" He tried to scoop her into his arms, but she stiffened and pulled away.

"It's not a matter of forgiveness, it's a matter of change. All I'm asking is for you to call if you're going to be late and let me know what's going on." She wanted to remain angry, to set him straight, but she could sense the rage dissipating. Simply being near him melted her resolve. "Is that too much to ask?"

"No, babes. Of course not. I guess I didn't know how much this was bothering you. I cross my heart and promise I won't do that again." He made an x over his heart with his finger, which was too endearing for words.

"Okay." She sighed. "I'll give you one more chance." She allowed him to take her into his arms and hold her, but an aching need for self protection kept her on her guard. Crazy about him, she didn't want to do anything to scare him away, but she didn't want to be taken advantage of either.

All at once she realized that she would have to compartmentalize her feelings about Damien if she were to remain in a relationship with him...and the thought of leaving him left her too raw to take seriously. She had to focus on his good points and try to separate out the downright hurtful behavior that gnawed at her. It was like having two men in one: the sweet, endearing, attentive lover and the selfish, neglectful, remorseless one. While she loved one of those men, she wasn't at all crazy about the other.

She hoped with all her heart the good Damien followed through with his promise because she wasn't at all certain she'd be able to stick to her threat if he didn't.

Chapter Ten

"My last session with Ellie was a difficult one," I tell the usual suspects at our clinical staff meeting, minus Cathy the social worker, who is on vacation.

"What happened?" her compadre Alice asks.

"It began with Ellie describing to me everything she had done to stay sober. She attended meetings regularly, found a sponsor, worked her steps and kept a journal and yet she was still struggling with the blank space in her mind where memory should reside. Her frustration was apparent. Although it wasn't the first time we had done this, I asked her if it would be all right for me take one more swipe at hypnotherapy with her. She eagerly agreed...

"Why don't you stretch out on the sofa," I said, "and when you're comfortable, close your eyes."

Ellie did as I suggested and once her eyes were closed, I asked her to take a couple of deep calming breaths. "Now Ellie, I want you to go back in your mind's eye to early evening on the night Jessica died and picture yourself back in the bar. Spend a few minutes replaying what happened before you blacked out.?"

As Ellie visualized that evening, I observed her rapid eye movement. "I can see it now. I was with Jessica. We chatted for a few minutes, but then she turned to speak to the man on her left. Since I had no one else to talk with, I turned to the guy on my right. The next thing I knew, a drink had been placed in front of me."

I jotted notes. "Can you remember anything about the man who was talking to Ellie? Did you listen in on their conversation or overhear anything? Was he familiar in anyway?"

"To be honest with you, I was so drunk I ignored him. I wouldn't recognize him in a police lineup if you paid me. I can't even remember

if I knew him or not. All I remember is being surprised that he bothered buying me a drink. Maybe Jessica had told him to. That's all I can figure."

"Ok. That's good. Now, can you recall anything else happening after that?"

Ellie shook her head from side to side and groaned. "It's all an empty screen. Even my flashbacks and nightmares can't fill in the gaping holes. No matter how hard I try, I can't recreate that night."

Tears of frustration dribbled across her cheek and soaked a spot on the sofa pillow.

"I feel for you. This is terribly difficult and I hate to press you further, but is there anything else you can remember?"

"I hate this!" she shouted. She thrust open her eyes and stared at me. "Damn it, Sarah! I hate the fact I keep drawing a blank. This isn't getting me anywhere."

I didn't know what more to say. A sense of failure and futility gnawed at me. I had used all the tools in my kit and I wasn't helping her to get any closer to the truth. I might even have been making it more problematic for her. Causing her to question the few flashes of memory she had acquired on her own. Faced with my limitations, a flock of birds took flight in my stomach.

"I feel like such a failure." I wrap my arms around myself.

"There, there, Sarah," Alice says, patting my shoulder. "We've all felt that way with difficult clients. Don't beat yourself up."

I sigh. The last thing I need is a pat on the back. I need direction. Skills. Creative thinking. Not comforting. "Does anyone have an idea of where I should go with this? I'm running out of steam."

Aaron crosses his arms over his chest in a commanding way. "Maybe it's time to throw in the towel with this case. There's not much else you can do to help her out."

I flinch. "I can't bow out on her without a fight. It wouldn't be fair to her."

"How about you?" he asks. "Is it fair for you to keep hitting your head against the same wall. That's a formula for burnout."

Of course, he's right, but I'm nowhere near burnout and I'm not about to ditch Ellie simply because I can't help her recall more of her fragmented memories. "I don't bail on clients that easily."

"Am I catching a whiff of co-dependency?" he asks with a knowing lift of his brow.

My anger flares so abruptly even I'm surprised by the extent of my reaction. I'm not about to let this arrogant son-of-a-bitch make me the problem and undermine my knowledge and authority. Why is he so determined I terminate Ellie? Since they're acquaintances, is he afraid I might stumble onto something he doesn't want me to know? "I resent being labeled like that. I'm doing the best job I can, and I'm not about to let you make me feel like a failure."

Sam lifts a hand. "You two squabbling isn't going to solve Ellie's problem. Lets get back to the solution. Since you still have a few more billable sessions left, maybe there's another way you can go about this. Any ideas?"

"Aaron had suggested trying truth serum at one time. I could use it when I place Ellie under hypnosis. It might be worth a try," I say. "As a psychologist I can't administer it myself, but you can. Would you be willing to work with me on this?"

"I've never tried it in a therapeutic situation, but I know it was used during the Second World War to help emotionally paralyzed soldiers with what they used to call Shell Shock, and is now referred to as Post Traumatic Stress Disorder. Not long ago I read that it's still being used in the UK to treat anxiety. In the article they mentioned Abbott Laboratory was the manufacturer. I can look into securing some for us."

Aaron releases a guffaw. "At this stage, it sounds like a desperate maneuver."

"It's highly unusual, but not necessarily out of the question," Sam adds. "I'm willing to research it and if it can help."

He rises. "That's enough for today. Lets reconvene at the same time, same station next week."

I stumble to my feet, to the sound of chairs scrapping the tile floor, and watch everyone head toward the door. I catch up with Aaron before he has a chance to exit the room and stop him with a hand on his arm. "Can I speak with you for a second?"

He looks annoyed. "I have a client in ten and I was hoping to take a break."

"No problem. I'll be quick."

He hangs back along with me and we wait until the others have filed from the room to speak.

"Okay, what is it?"

"Why didn't you mention you knew Ellie before you ran into her?"

He blanches. "I only knew her briefly as a friend of Jessica, who always called her Ellinor. It's an honest mistake. I never put two and two together."

"Ellie tells me you dated Jessica for awhile. Did you not put that together either?"

"You never mentioned Jessica's name. You kept referring to her as Ellie's friend. I had no idea. I was shocked about what happened to Jessica. It was devastating."

If it is, his eyes don't reveal his anguish. "Does your relationship with Jessica have anything to do with your sudden change of heart about treating Ellie with Sodium Pentothal?"

He blanched. "Of course not."

"Really? I only hope you won't let your relationship with either of these women color your role in consulting with me on this case, or I'd like you to recuse yourself from the conference."

He laughs. "You have to be kidding. Recuse myself? What is this? An Act of Congress or a court of law? You're being overly dramatic. I wasn't involved with Jessica for long, and I hardly knew Ellinor. I can be fully objective in giving you feedback."

He starts to back out of the room. "I have to run. Don't make a mountain out of a molehill. Let's do our jobs and do them well."

Before I have a chance to say anything else, he's hurrying down the hall. I stare at his back. In light of his antagonist behavior in this case, I don't trust him or his motivation. I'll keep that in mind when he gives me direction or advice.

I let myself into my condo in Queen Village. Unsettled the entire way home from the clinic after my encounter with Aaron, I'm still a bit unnerved when I arrive. The moment I enter the apartment, I notice a piece of paper on the floor by my desk and suspect something's wrong. Then my eyes alight on the cat, stretched out on the floor by the desk, and wonder if she knocked it off by accident.

Still the sense of unease follows me into the bedroom as I change into a pair of black tights and a long white tee shirt. Maybe I'm being unduly paranoid after my earlier encounter. I hope that's all it is.

To quell my concerns, I heat a cup of tea. A soothing cup of chamomile almost always works wonders, but today it does little to quiet the buzz of electrical energy racing along my nerve endings. Since I'm too tired to take a walk, I chose a meditation disc for a short centering session.

In the bedroom, I'm about to switch on the sound meditation disc, when I notice something unusual. I could have sworn I had closed the laptop lid when I left in the morning, but it is noticably open now. Like a magnet, it draws me over. I stare at it open-mouthed. Even though it is a common practice of mine to close the computer, perhaps in my rush I'd forgotten it today. Perhaps...but not likely.

The tingle of nerves morph into a vibration. I lower myself to the bed. Has someone been on my laptop, checking into my personal data? And is that someone Drew? It wouldn't surprise me. Not only is Drew perpetually determined to locate Rachel, but he's clever enough and sneaky enough to pull off this kind of intrusion, although he rarely misses a detail, like leaving the cover open. It isn't outside the realm of possibilities that he found his way into my condo and onto my computer without leaving much in the way of evidence. The idea he might have been in my home when I wasn't around didn't sit well with me at all.

And how about the search history? Maybe he isn't so clever that he completely covered his tracks. He might have left evidence on the computer. I boot it up and notice the last thing viewed was my email account. Again, my nerves jangle.

Rachel's revised email address was in my address book. What could Drew do with that knowledge? Is there a way to do reverse lookup from email to home address? I don't know, but I have to find out. In the meantime, I'll have to alert Rachel to the danger. The last thing she needs with the new toddler is complications from Drew. The last thing either of us need is Drew in our lives...period!

Before doing anything else, I email Rachel and let her know Drew might have gotten into my file and may have found her email. I also ring her and leave a phone message. That's all I can do for now.

Afterwards, I call Lara. With the likelihood Drew gained access to my condo, remaining alone isn't an option. I have to get out of here. While I don't want to worry Lara, I need a safe place to spend the night, or I will never be able to sleep. In the morning, I'll take time off from work to find a locksmith to replace my lock and add a deadbolt. I'll live Fort Knox style if necessary. I'm determined to protect myself from Drew, no matter what I have to do. Not only is he a relentless psychopath, but he's the smartest one I've ever met.

And the most dangerous.

Chapter Eleven

Ellie

After work, Ellie stopped by the market to buy the fixings for a steak dinner. Damien had promised to be over earlier than usual that evening to celebrate their third month anniversary. Besides the steaks, she purchased arugula for the salad and russet potatoes to make a casserole. Excited about the prospect of a romantic evening, she scurried home, but about halfway there again had the sensation of being watched. She hastened her footsteps, relieved when she slammed the door behind her.

After taking ten minutes to debrief, which included surveilling her street from the living room window, she finally felt collected enough to toss the potato casserole together and chop vegetables for the salad. Job done, she put the oven on and made her way to the bedroom to dress. She changed into a black sheaf she kept for special occasions and she added high heels and silver chains. She appraised herself in the mirror, pleased at her appearance.

After washing her face and applying foundation and lipstick, she put the casserole in the oven, tossed the salad and readied the steaks to be grilled when Damien arrived. Since he was already a few minutes later than he said he'd be, she turned on the news and took a seat on the sofa. An hour later, she turned off the oven, took off her make-up, dress and heels and put on jeans and a tee. Damien had done it again. He had managed to spoil her dinner even after all her effort. Disappointment coursed through her veins.

He arrived a couple of minutes after she reclaimed her seat on the sofa. Rather than rise, she sat, staring at the tv, when he entered the apartment. He approached her.

"Sorry, I was held up."

She pouted. "Where the heck have you been?"

He cocked his head boyishly, which was normally appealing to her. Not now. "What's the matter? I'm not that late, am I?"

He had forgotten all about their plans. How could he be so cavalier? "I can't believe you forgot our date tonight. Don't you care about me at all?"

He struck his forehead with the palm of his hand. "Oh my God, I'm so sorry. I spaced out our dinner. When Chuck asked me to take care of locking up the office, I said I would."

"I went through a lot of trouble to plan a special meal for you, but you don't give a damn about me, do you?"

"How can you say that? Of course, I care about you."

She shook her head. "What do they say, actions speak louder than words. Well, if that's the case, your actions say you don't give a damn."

He came over and kneeled by the sofa. "Don't say that. It isn't true."

"I'm so tired of being treated this way. I don't know if I can take anymore." She swatted away the hand that reached for her. "Leave me alone. I've had enough of you!"

He stood and stared at her. "Get over it, Ellie. I have to work for a living. I can't be at your beck and call all the time.

"Or any of the time."

"I don't have to tolerate your insecurity any longer. If you want me out of your life, I'm on my way." He pivoted on his heels and marched toward the door.

All at once the rage dissipated, replaced with panic. The last thing she wanted to do was alienate Damien. She only had one prior boyfriend in her entire life, and never one with such good looks and charisma. Was she a fool? What was she thinking? She would do anything to hold onto him. "Don't go!" she shouted.

He had been reaching for the door and methodically turned his head to look back at her. "Why not? You don't want me here."

"I didn't mean it. I was hurt and angry. I'm sorry. I shouldn't have said what I did."

He rested his head in his hand, like Rodin's *The Thinker* on the Benjamin Franklin Parkway, as though considering what to do. "To tell the truth, I'm getting tired of these scenes. You can't decide what you want. As much as I care about you, I can't keep doing this."

"Okay. Okay. If it bothers you that much, I'll stop."

"That's easy for you to say, but I need to know that this won't keep happening. You knew from the moment we met I had a demanding job that often requires me to stay late at work. I supervise others and have to make sure everything is wrapped tight at night before I go home. I have a lot of responsibility and can't always be on your schedule."

Her heart beat rapidly; sweat coated her palms. Of course, he had explained all that upfront and it hadn't been a problem for her at first. She could kick herself for being so needy and sensitive. The last thing she wanted was to scare him away, but she found herself doing the exact opposite of what she desired. She had to get a grip on herself. "I know it's no use saying I'm sorry again, but I'll do my best not to be so reactive. I don't want to lose you. I love you."

She had said it. She watched for his reaction with intense anxiety. Would her admission please him or piss him off?

"I don't know. You have problems." He looked away as though contemplating what to do, then back at her. "All right, but no more fireworks for no good reason. I need you to be more supportive, or what's the use of a relationship? Life's tough enough without making it more difficult for one another. Right?"

Yes, of course, he was right. She wanted to be a loving partner and not a nag. She would have to handle her anxieties and insecurities without bringing him in on it. Perhaps Al Anon would help. Whatever happened, she would make a commitment to herself never to question him again. She would become the type of woman he wanted to be around even if it killed her.

On Saturday morning Ellie awoke early to be at the Unitarian Church before anyone else arrived. She dressed in her black sheaf with a tailored black jacket and black pumps. She had invited Damian along, but after apologizing profusely, he explained he had to work that day. Disappointed he wouldn't be by her side, she would have to find solace in the few friends she and Jessica shared as well as Jessica's wonderful brother, Brandon.

At ten forty-five, people began arriving at the church. Jack had taken over organizing the pulpit and left her to greet the guests as they appeared. Brandon was one of the first and gave Ellie a big hug before taking a seat below the platform in the front row. Jack had already saved himself a seat next to Brandon's with Ellie on his other side. Slowly the chapel filled with a coterie of Jessica's friends, a group of family members and a smattering of co-workers.

Glancing around, she could only sense the futility of it all. Jessica had been such a shining light in her life...and the life of others...but only a small group of friends and relatives had bothered to attend her memorial. It made Ellie consider the sacrifices she had made for others. While she had always been a caretaker, she questioned whether it had been worth her effort to please them, often at her own expense. As they say, and what was especially true in Jessica's case, "life is short". Perhaps it was time to take care of herself for a change.

Her watch showed 11:10; the service scheduled to begin at 11:15. She spotted Aaron Davis enter the rear of the room. Surprised, because she hadn't expected him to make an appearance at Jessica's memorial, she watched him take a seat. He flinched when she caught his eye, as though he hadn't wanted to be seen, but graciously smiled back at her. At the sound of the minister's voice, she turned around to face the podium.

The service went smoothly with the Minister praising Jessica, even though he didn't know her, and calling on Brandon, then Jack and finally Ellie to make their remarks. When it was her turn, Ellie read from a prepared statement, but could hardly see the words through her tears. She spoke about all the fun times she and Jessica had had together and how much she missed her beautiful and adventuresome friend. She chocked up repeatedly, forced to stop intermittently and regain her composure.

Even in the midst of the pain, a small niggling idea took root. No matter what she said to the congregation, she suddenly recognized the shallow nature of her friendship with Jessica. As often as they had been together, as much as they had shared, she knew so little about her friend, except what she saw on the surface. Most of their evenings were spent drinking together and, even when they spoke of personal problems or social concerns, it was always under the influence. Alcohol had dictated the depth of their relationship and had prevented it from becoming more intimate or meaningful. She regretted having lost the chance to know this lovely lady. At this recognition, the tears flowed more freely.

The service ended when the congregation rose and sang Amazing Grace as one. Again, she choked back tears brought on by grief.

Afterwards, a table set up with coffee and Jessica's favorite chocolate croissants provided a gathering place for a few minutes of communion and comfort. She took the time to swap tales of Jessica's exploits with friends, before she spied Aaron heading toward the exit. She caught up with him before he could slink out the door.

"I'm so glad you were able to attend. I hope you'll have a croissant before you go."

Aaron shook his head. "Sorry, but I have to run." He started toward the exit, but before reaching the tall double doors, pivoted toward her. "That was a beautiful service. I know Jessica would have loved it."

How well had he known Jessica? Ellie would have liked to know more about their relationship, but this was not the time to ask. "How did you hear about the memorial?"

He didn't have a easy answer so he shuffled his feet for a few seconds. "Jessica and I had a mutual friend, but this friend is a private practice client so I'm not at liberty to break her anonymity. She's the one who told me."

"Oh," Ellie said, but she couldn't help wondering who that mutual friend could be and why no one had mentioned that Aaron was on the guest list. Was this for real? "I'm glad you could make it. Jessica would have appreciated your being here."

Aaron scoffed. "I'm not so sure of that." He backed away before she had a chance to ask for an explanation. "Gotta run. See you soon." And he was gone, leaving her with too many questions and too few answers.

Chapter Twelve

Although it takes a couple hours for me to completely calm myself after the incident at home, being around Lara, Dicky and Will distracts me enough that I can finally concentrate on something other than the apparent break in. Will, always the talker, entertains me at dinner with tales of his co-workers at the law firm, a motley crew if there ever was one; and Lara, always the consummate hostess, plies me with beef bourguignon and grilled asparagus. Even Dicky is on his best behavior, spending most of his time playing video games on a tablet, but he breaks away to voluntarily give me a kiss before being sent off to bed.

Satiated in both stomach and spirit, I wander into the guest room to read. Not long after I crawl into bed, Lara knocks on the door and lets herself into the room. "Sarah, are you okay? I'm a little worried about you."

No matter how I behave, there is no way to fool Lara. "I'm fine."

Lara gives me a knowing grin. "Didn't you tell me that stands for freaked out, insecure, neurotic, and emotional?"

No use even trying. "I don't know, maybe it's just fear, but I have a feeling Drew's on my tail."

Lara's grunts. "Oh, no..."

"But I'm really okay...only...a bit concerned."

"What's with this 'bit.' We're talking about the asshole who almost killed you. You're minimizing this as always."

I tent my hands and lower my chin to them. I'm not sure how much to tell Lara. I don't want to worry her unnecessarily, but I can use her support. "You're right, I'm worried, but there's not much else I can do. I plan to add a new deadbolt on my condo and get a can of mace, but what other options do I have?"

"Move in with us for awhile."

I pat the bed for Lara to take a seat. "I love you so much, sis, but there's no way I want to move in on you right now. You have enough on your hands. Besides, I don't want to rely on anyone else. I'm certain I can figure out how to take care of myself."

"With that psycho on the loose. I'm not so sure..."

Neither am I. "Remember, I'm older sister and I'm the one who should be taking care of you."

"Yeah, but you're the one in harm's way. I don't like this one bit. This jerk is a serious threat to you. I can't see you being on your own. I'd worry about you all the tim–"

It's nice to know I'm loved, but I don't want to be smothered. "Listen, I don't want to worry you because I need you to be a source of strength for me, not a sniveling sister. Please pull it together and be my rock. I need one right now."

Lara studies her hands for the longest time, but I let her be. She needs space...enough space to allow her head to take over where her heart had gone. All emotion and no reason would only prove a problem for us both. "All right, but the offer's always open."

I take her hand in mind. "Thanks."

"I know you'll never take me up on it. So, I want you to contact me everyday, no matter if it's only to say hi and goodbye."

"Of course. I promise to call you daily. I don't want you to fret about me."

"Too late to prevent that."

"Sorry. I didn't mean to frighten you."

"With that loon on the loose, anything is possible. I don't even want to consider what he might do."

Neither did I. "Remember he's after my former client, not me. He has no use for me at all with her out of the picture. I can't see why he'd bother."

"I hope you're right. He came after you as a way to get to her before, I don't see why he wouldn't do it again."

"Lets hope he's gotten over her and moved on. He's a good looking guy and I've heard a lot of lonely-heart crazies wrote to him in prison. Perhaps he hooked up with one of them."

That seems to cheer Lara a little. She smiles. "It would be what he deserved, wouldn't it?"

"It sure would. Now how about a small slice of that cheesecake I saw on the kitchen counter?"

"With decaf?"

"Sounds like a plan." I only wish I had a plan to deal with Drew.

But I don't.

"I've been in contact with Abbott Laboratories," Sam announces at the start of the next staff meeting, "and am looking into the possibility of purchasing enough Sodium Pentothal for a treatment dose as well as specific directions from one of their researchers on how to administer it."

This pronouncement is encouraging. "Great. I've been stuck on what I should do with Ellie. This is good news."

"I guess that means there hasn't been much progress this week." Aaron wears what looks to me like a smirk, but might be an encouraging smile.

"You're right. And since there's nothing new to discuss about Ellie this week, I'd like to take the opportunity to address Cathy's questions about treating alcoholic patients."

Cathy lights up. "I saw my first alcoholic patient a few days ago and stopped by Sarah's office for some guidance. I don't know a lot about treating alcoholics."

Aaron rifles through a sheaf of paper and looked uninterested, but both social workers are staring at me with expectant expressions.

Ignoring Aaron in favor of the others, I continue. "As you all know alcoholism is a chronic disease of unestablished origin. There are those who believe it's genetic in nature, but new research points to early childhood trauma, ranging from loss to abandonment, or neglect to serious abuse and everything in between, as the real culprit. According to the research, the reason it runs in families is because they pass the trauma on one generation to the next, therefore, passing on the tendency toward alcoholism or other emotional and physical illnesses."

"What hope is there in treating alcoholics, if they're stuck in a perpetuating cycle of family dysfunction?" Cathy asks, appearing defeated.

"The only hope for alcoholics to recover is if they hit the proverbial bottom and become willing to seek treatment. There are people in Alcoholics Anonymous who have been sober for fifty years or more, but at one point in time they accepted the First Step of the Twelve Step program and admitted they were powerless over alcohol and that their lives had become unmanageable."

"Why do they have to hit a bottom to seek help?" Alice asked. "If I knew I had cancer, I wouldn't wait until it had spread to my lungs to make an appointment with an Oncologist. Why would I?"

"Of course not. But alcoholism is an insidious disease. Every time an alcoholic takes a drink, they are damaging their central nervous system and this leads to distorted thinking and inappropriate emotional response. As part of that distortion, the defense mechanism of denial takes over and convinces the sufferer that the drug is not their problem. It's difficult, if not almost impossible, for them to admit to themselves they are powerless over the substance until it's late in the process. For some, too late. The majority of alcoholics never achieve long-term recovery and most of them will end up dying either directly or indirectly from their disease."

"Wow!" Cathy makes a face. "How can we help them if they refuse to admit to their problem?"

"That's a good question; one that friends and family members of the alcoholic have been asking for years. The good news is that this "bottom" has been raised in recent years by education and awareness. Often alcoholics get the help they need through their families, their jobs or the court system. And there are ways we can help to accelerate their bottom."

"Accelerate their bottom," Aaron scoffs. "How the hell can you do that? Pour the booze down their throats?"

He knows better than that. I bristle. "Shy of that, we can do an intervention. Confront them with the reality of their disease and how it's affected their lives and the lives of those around them. Bringing in significant others can help. Spouses, children, parents, bosses, friends. All these people can serve as witness to the demolition derby their lives have become."

"Is that the only option we have?" Alice asked.

"Members of Alcoholics Anonymous can also help. They're always willing to send a member over to speak to one of our patients. As they say in AA, it's one member helping another, and they're often the best sales people for sobriety because they're alcoholics, but they're living productive and happy lives."

"Not everyone is willing to go to AA.," Sam chimes in. "I've had patients who refuse to attend 'those meetings'. In that case, we can use a chemical intervention, such as Antabuse, where the drug stops the alcoholic from drinking by making them ill instead of making them high. It can be effective in some instances, but the best medicine is a willingness on the part of the drinker to do what they can to stop the addictive and destructive behavior."

"I still don't fully grasp if alcoholism is a disease or if it's another compulsive behavior trait disguised as an illness," Aaron says, sardonically. "Doesn't calling this a disease take away all responsibility from the alcoholic?"

"In a way, but it also frees the alcoholic to either rely on a Power greater than themselves and a fellowship like AA to help them stay sober, or to find another solution. The fact is the alcoholic is truly powerless over their compulsion. It's only by turning their life and will over to something more powerful than themselves that they let go of trying to control everybody and everything, which is a symptom of the disease. Unfortunately, when someone grows up in a dysfunctional family, which is not uncommon in alcoholic households, and then spends their life unable to limit their own drinking, or curtail the damage it wreaks in their life, they are forever after consumed with the need to control everyone and everything around them. It is this behavioral trait more than any other that gets the alcoholic in trouble. Learning to accept reality and let go of the outcome of events, which is referred to as surrender, can lead to a serenity and a happiness the alcoholic has never known. This is what keeps them coming back to a program of recovery."

I glance at my watch. "Oops, it's time for me to keep coming back...to work, that is. I have a client in a few minutes, so that's all for today, folks. I hope what I shared will begin to clarify the mechanism of alcoholism and help all of us to do more effective work with our alcoholic patients. We can discuss this difficult disease further as Ellie's treatment progresses."

"Any excuse to avoid questions," Aaron says with a sneer.

I ignore him, excuse myself, and take off at a trot for my office, all the while wondering why Aaron always has to be so recalcitrant. His attitude not only irks me, but makes my job far more difficult to perform. His hostility toward me bares all the marks of resentment and jealousy.

In AA they define insanity as doing the same thing and expecting different results. Am I insane staying at this clinic under these circumstances, and would I be better off in my own practice again? Even with this apprehension, I immediately reconsider. As daunting as Aaron's anger can be, with Drew on the loose, there's no way I will be returning to private practice any time soon.

Chapter Thirteen

Ellie

Not long after the memorial, Jack began to avoid her. Ellie tried calling him on more than one occasion, but he failed to return any of her calls. Funny, he had always been so responsive in the past, why the sudden change of heart? Could it be her sobriety made her far less fun to be around, or could it be something else? Maybe he didn't want to be reminded of Jessica, or maybe he had something to hide.

She had mentioned Jack's behavior to Damien over lunch at a local coffee shop not far from her apartment one sticky, hot Saturday in late June. As soon as she mentioned the issue with Jack, Damien was all over it.

"From what you told me, I never trusted that guy. Maybe it was his drinking that put me off, but he wasn't a straight shooter."

She stared out the window at the street, busy with Saturday morning joggers and people walking their dogs. How lovely everything looked in summer. The oak and elm trees lining the street were in full bloom. Rows of brick town homes, many with historic plaques, displayed garden boxes overflowing with crimson geraniums, bright yellow marigolds and orange day Lilies. "I don't know about that, but he certainly hasn't been available lately."

Damien took a hit of his double latte. "Yeah, well I don't think he sounds trustworthy."

Unusual for Damien to badmouth anyone, especially someone he only knew through her, she suddenly had the urge to jump in and defend Jack, but what could she say. After what Jack had told her about Jessica, Damien might be onto something. "That might be true, but his rejection still bothers me. You don't realize what good friends we were when Jessica was alive. I'm really hurt."

He reached across the table and took her hand in his. "I'm sorry the SOB has hurt you so much."

It felt so good to be supported. She squeezed Damien's hand. "It's such a lovely day. Lets talk about something more uplifting."

"Okay, how about if you were to tell me more about your therapy. Hank asked me how it's been going for you, but I had trouble answering. It's been a big secret."

With his head cocked to the side, he looked boyish and adorable. "There's not much to tell. I still can't remember a thing about the night Jessica died, and nothing Sarah's tried has stirred up any new memory."

"What has she done?"

Ellie couldn't help but be flattered by his interest. While his work kept him away most of the week and they hardly had any time together, she wanted to keep him engaged. "Mainly talk therapy and hypnosis. She mentioned truth serum..."

Damien made a face. "Truth serum? That's weird."

"Yeah, but I'm willing to try anything." She released his hand to spread cream cheese on her bagel. "Now it's your turn to tell me something about you. I haven't seen much of you this last week. What's going on?"

Damien stiffened. His being unavailable had become such a sore subject, he immediately became defensive if she brought it up. No matter how hard she tried to suppress her feelings and avoid the topic, nothing stopped her from mentioning it even when she didn't intend to.

"I hope we're not belaboring that one again."

"I only want to know how you're doing and what you're up to when we're apart?"

"Same old. Same old. Nothing much to report. It's all work and no play."

His reticence to speak about himself always bothered her. How could they become more intimate if their relationship was so one-sided. "There has to be more to your life than you're telling me. Come on. Give me some dirt."

"That's about all there was to my week...dirt. I had to cover for one guy at work who quit unexpectedly, and do the job of two others who were slacking off. I should be paid for both of them. I have no say in who's hired and who's fired. It's a frustrating situation, but I hate to lay all that on you."

"Lay it on me, please. I want to know what's going on. It's no bother at all."

"Okay," he said. "I'll do that, but not now. Like you said, it's too pretty a day. Why don't we go to a museum or shopping, or do anything besides sitting around talking about my problems."

"Only if you tell me one more thing about your week. Then I'll go."

"All right." He stared at something over her head. "I've been considering quitting my job."

Even on the heels of his disillusionment, that was the last thing she expected. "Really?"

"Well, not right away. I'd have to have a backup plan."

"Like what?"

"Another job. I might start looking around."

Her heart sank. She calculated how much more time his job search would take away from her and realized it would mean seeing him even less of him than she already did. "How can you manage that? You have such little free time."

"That's been the holdup, but I have no choice. I have a few days paid sick and vacation leave which I might have to use."

Her sense of elation at being with him quickly dissipated. In her calculation, this might be one of their last chances to be together for weeks to come.

He finished his coffee and stood. "Come on, you promised we'd do something fun. Lets figure out what it is."

She stared into his bright blue eyes, but for once that didn't mollify her sense of loss. The more she had of him, the more she wanted, but the less she got. And the more she ached for him. Sometimes she even wondered if he was spending his time with other women and not at work as he claimed. Or doing other activities which he preferred over being with her. The thought made her sick to her stomach.

She gave him her hand and he pulled her to her feet.

"All right lets go," she said, but only half-heartedly because the more time she spent with him today, the less time he'd have for her tomorrow.

And the less satisfied she would be.

Sunday morning Damien reported he had to go into work for a few hours and left soon after wolfing down a bowl of cereal. With time to kill and nothing planned, Ellie took Locust Street to the Schuykill River Boardwalk. While this wasn't the first time she had taken the new trail, it still gave her a thrill to be strolling along the river with the city rising in bas relief behind her. Although the day hung heavy, more overcast and muggy than Saturday, she enjoyed meandering along the Schuylkill River, passing kids walking beside their parents and dogs led on leashes as couples and families enjoyed this recently completed attraction.

Watching all the activity made her feel lonelier than she had anticipated and thoughts of Damien filled her mind. Although disappointed with his long absences and lack of attentiveness, she couldn't fathom the thought of leaving him. Merely speculating about it caused an intense ache and called her attention to the power he held over her heart. The last thing she wanted to face was the suffering his loss would create.

Distracted by her ruminations, she was startled when Mary M from her noon meeting called he name.

Mary caught up with her, beaming as though seeing her was the best thing that had happened all day. And maybe it was, because it was the best thing that had happened to Ellie.

"Isn't this terrific," Mary gushed. "I never expected to run into you out here."

"I'm always running into someone from our meeting."

"I was hoping to have company for the walk. Are you headed toward the South Street bridge? Do you mind my joining you?"

It might distract her from her worries. "Sure, why not."

Mary walked by Ellie's side. "Funny I should run into you today after seeing Damien."

Ellie's antennae went up. "Oh, where was that?"

"He stopped into the morning meeting, but didn't stay long."

"That's strange, because he told me he had to be at work by ten."

"Well, if he did, he must have been late since the meeting didn't start until 10:30."

Ellie had a funny feeling in the pit of her stomach. This wasn't adding up at all. Why had he lied to her? Was he avoiding her? Or was there another reason? "This has been fun, but I just remembered I have to be at a friend's house for lunch. I better get going."

Mary looked stunned. "You sure? Couldn't we go a little bit further?"

"You go ahead. I have to head back to my car or I'll be late. Toodles." She took off at a clip for Locust Street, waiting until Mary was out of sight before she dialed Damien's number. He answered on the third ring.

"What's going on?"

"I was going to ask you the same thing. I ran into Mary M. and she told me you were at the meeting this morning. You said you had to be at work by ten."

The silence at the other end of the line spoke volumes. Dread filled her.

"I'm so tired of this interrogation. I don't owe you an explanation. I can run my own life without your damn help!"

The line went dead.

Feeling as if she'd been slapped in the face, tears sprang into her eyes. She couldn't believe he would hang up on her. How disrespectful.

Hurt and angry, it took her a few minutes to feel the fear. But when it came, it was crippling. She could barely breath. Doubled over, she must have been a sight because a jogger stared at her as he passed by. Thank goodness the look on her face must have prevented him from offering help. She didn't want to explain what was going on to anyone.

Gathering up the courage, she was about to call Damien back, when the phone rang and his name appeared on the screen. Still stung by his behavior, she decided to let it go to voicemail.

She listened to the message.

Hi babes. Listen, I'm really sorry for what I said and how I behaved. You know I have a thing about being questioned and it always sets me off. I didn't mean to hang up on you. I merely reacted. And, yes, I was supposed to go to work at ten, but Mike called and said he wouldn't be there until eleven, so I had a few minutes to stop by the meeting. That's all. It was as innocent as it sounds. So, lets talk later, but please don't be upset. I need you to forgive me. Click.

Ellie listened to the message a second time because hearing his voice calmed the storm raging inside. As angry as she was and as justified as she felt, it wouldn't be long before she forgave him. No matter what he did, or how he behaved, she couldn't hold onto a resentment for long. And even if she did, she'd never risk the result of his wrath.

Chapter Fourteen

Sarah

No matter where I've gone these last few weeks, I've had the sense of being followed. Nothing concrete, mind you, but a pervasive vibe of eyes on me. Yet, when I scan my surroundings, I see nothing out of the ordinary. Perhaps it's only anxiety on my part, but when I leave my apartment, my skin crawls with anticipation of trouble to come.

Because of this, I have started to take alternative ways to work, which, with traffic, often make me late. Today I arrived ten minutes later than expected and Sam was standing in the lobby, pointing at his watch with a wry expression. Although it seemed good natured enough, I don't want to create any problems. I promised myself I would leave earlier in the future rather than take any chances.

So, when I'm called into Sam's office, I'm expecting the worst. With moist palms and mild cramps, I contritely approach his large oak desk. "You rang?" I say in an attempt to lighten the mood.

He glances up from his paperwork and with a sweep of his hand indicates a chair. "Take a seat."

I follow orders. "Is everything okay?" What an inane question, but I need to know if it isn't.

Sam signs a letter and places it in an envelope. "I was able to secure a dose of Triopenal Sodium...you know, Sodium Pentothal...large enough to treat your patient."

I almost sigh out loud with relief. "That's great."

"Now we have to arrange a time when she's available to schedule an examination room with Thomas Jefferson Hospital. Can you come up with a couple different days and times when you're both free?"

"Ellie's scheduled appointment time on Friday afternoon would certainly work. I believe she takes off of work early on Friday and is open most of the afternoon. Let me check with her and I'll be back with you about it by tomorrow."

"Okay, that will do. I've never done this type of treatment before, but Abbott laboratories gave me specfic instructions on how to administer it. I'm curious about how it works."

"Me, too. Fingers crossed it makes a real difference for Ellie. I've noticed that she's feeling more and more threatened by her amnesia."

"Threatened? Why's that?"

"She believes whoever is to blame for Jessica's death may come back for her."

"The blackout has certainly left her in a vulnerable place." Sam stands. "This is a serious matter and I hate to cut you short, but I have an administrative meeting right now. Let's talk later, but, in the meantime, let me know when you want me to schedule the room."

He walks me to the office door. "I'm so grateful you're willing to attempt this novel treatment with me. I don't know if many Administrators would be so willing to try something this revolutionary. You're a good guy, Doc."

"We'll see how highly you think of me if this doesn't work."

"You have that wrong. It's not about whether we're successful or not, even though I hope we are. It's about who you are as a doctor and a boss that impresses me." He gazes into my eyes in a way he never has before and I can sense my face heat. "I'll see you later." I bolt from the office before he notices my reaction. I like this man, maybe a little too much. I didn't intend to wax too sentimental with him, even though I meant ever word I said.

The next time I see Sam is at the weekly staff meeting.

"So here's the arrangements." Sam combs fingers through his thinning brown hair. "We can use one of the rooms in the urgent care area where we'll have access to the IV machine as well as monitors to measure the patient's response. I will have to be present in the exam room, but the rest of you can watch us through a one way mirror with the patient's permission."

Aaron looks as bored as ever. "What do you hope to gain from this?"

To back Sam, I pipe up, "Unless you come up with a different option, what do we have to lose by trying out chemical therapy? We only have a limited amount of time to work with this patient so we're doing everything we can."

He raises a brow. "You're wasting everyone's time and the hospital's money."

"Let's hope not," Sam replies. "This might be our last chance to break through the fog of her blackout."

"Good luck," Aaron says. "I did my research and there aren't any success stories."

Suddenly, my suspicion is triggered. Why has Aaron been doing research on this case? It isn't his patient or his concern. "What kind of research?

"I checked out the results of medication induced hypnosis online and in a couple of medical journals to learn if it had been efficacious in retrieving memory in blackout cases."

Something seems wrong here. His motivation doesn't compute. "I'm surprised with all your patients you had the time to research mine."

He shrugs. "It piqued my interest. I've never dealt with a situation like this one and I wanted to know what we were getting into."

"We? She's not your patient."

"But she's a patient of County Mental Health. It effects us all. And besides, there is always something I can learn that might eventually be useful."

I don't buy his argument, but I'm getting nowhere fast. No use debating him further at this time.

"So, let's all meet in the urgent care area prior to the treatment on Friday at 1:45. We can regroup there and prepare for what will follow," Sam says, cutting off the argument. "It's time to move on to the next patient. Alice you have a case you wish to discuss."

I listen to Alice describe a Borderline Personality Disorder, but my mind keeps drifting back to Aaron's behavior. I can't help feeling he has overstepped his boundaries and has taken a more active roll in this case than would be required or appreciated. And I can't help wondering why.

A hush falls over the exam room as Sam prepares Ellie for the procedure. She has agreed to allow the staff to observe from behind a one-way mirror and the consultation staff has reconvened in the adjacent room. Even Aaron, who insisted he should be present in the main room since he knew Ellie and could encourage her, reluctantly joined the rest of the group. Luckily Sam intervened in that conflict and made it clear no one would be present in the room beyond the active participants in the process.

Ellie appears nervous, wringing her hands, but I reassure her Sam knows what he's doing and she will be actively monitored through every step of the procedure. Sam busies himself hooking up a machine to monitor her vital signs, then inserts the IV. He asks Ellie to close her eyes and take a couple of deep breaths. At that, he switches on the intravenous drip.

I can watch on the monitors when her blood pressure dips and pulse declines. It becomes obvious the sedative is kicking in. When I'm confident she's ready, I proceed with the session, leaving the medical end of it to Sam.

I pull a chair alongside the exam table. "Take a couple of deep breaths through your nose and release them through your mouth." After hearing Ellie exhale a second time, I continue, "Now I want you to go back to the evening of March 26th just before you left work to meet Jessica at the club and tell me what you're experiencing."

Ellie's silent for a long moment. Then I hear her mumble, "I'm excited and nervous. I go into the bathroom to reapply my makeup and, while looking at myself in the mirror, I feel a flush of euphoria and anticipation about the evening ahead. I love to go out Friday evenings for Happy Hour. It's marks the end of the week and the beginning of the weekend. It means a break in my routine. A chance at romance. All bubbly and buddies." Even though there's a slight slur to her words, I am able to jot down what she's saying almost as fast as she can say it.

"Go on."

"I take my hair out of the bun it's been in all day and brush it out. Then I apply rouge and lipstick. One more glance in the mirror and I experience the rush of readiness. It's party time." She's aglow with feeling, which brightens her sallow complexion. "I have changed into heels and a form-fitting, peach-colored spandex top and I check myself in the mirror before I leave for the club. When I arrive, Jessica is sitting at the bar with Jack. After I join them, he rises, gives me a quick hug and rushes off to the dance-floor with a blonde he picks up along the way, leaving me alone with Jessica. We have a couple of stiff drinks, toasting our weekend of fun and freedom before a guy appears on Jessica's far side. I hear him order us both another of the martinis we are having. The bartender delivers the drinks, but I don't notice when because I have already started to speak with the guy on my right."

"Could you see and identify the man who bought your martini?" I ask.

She shakes her head. "No...no, Jessica sat between us...I never saw him and, to be frank, I didn't care to. Men were always hitting on Jessica and buying us drinks. To me they were anonymous."

"What happened next?"

"All I remember is Jessica passing the drink to me and my taking a few sips...then everything went blank..."

"Can you see anything else?"

"Shit!" she says suddenly. "Damn it! I can't remember a thing....I went under fast... I've often wondered if it was the alcohol or if I was drugged. I don't know what hit me...but I want to know...I want to remember...why can't I..."

To calm her, I take her hand in mine. "Don't pressure yourself. Relax and see if anything else comes to you."

Tears gather in the corners of her eyes. "I want this to work...I want this to work...I want this to work..."

I wipe the tears with a tissue. "Don't torment yourself. The harder you push yourself the less likely we'll get results. Try to take a couple of deep breaths and calm ..."

Sam signals me with a thumb up he is increasing the dosage. Within minutes, Ellie becomes less coherent and rambles on about her mother. She explains in a whiney tone how she didn't feel close to her mom, but was closer to her dad, who wasn't around much of the time...how her autistic baby brother came along and took all of her mother's attention and on and on and on. Even with my prompting and direction, she meanders from one subject to another, not necessarily in any sequential fashion. When I attempt to direct her back to the evening in question, she quickly loses her train of thought and tells me about her bad experiences being bullied in middle school.

I pull Sam aside and ask him to decrease the dose, hoping that as she withdraws, Ellie will become more focused and more compliant, but that doesn't happen. She continues her stream-of-consciousness mutterings without any real purpose or design. Every time I try to bring her back to the night in question, she deviates off onto other issues. She mentions frustration with her boyfriend Damien and her job, but nothing further surfaces related to Jessica's death.

Not long after her withdrawal from the Sodium Pentothal, lucidity returns. Sam departs after making certain her blood pressure, heartbeat and respirations are within normal range and removing the IV and monitors, but I remain by her side until she is more fully alert.

She lifts herself slowly to a sitting position on the exam table, tears again filling her eyes. "I couldn't do it, could I? I'm such a failure. I don't know what to do."

I wrap my arms around her and give her a squeeze. "You did what you could do, nothing more and nothing less. You accepted a big risk by undergoing a technique that's totally unproven. It took a tremendous amount of courage on your part. You should pat yourself on the back."

"Maybe I would if I wasn't so discouraged. Nothing I've done has revealed what happened that night. This is a total dead-end."

"Are you giving up on me? Because I'm not ready to give up on you. Please reconsider. This might not have been the breakthrough we were hoping for, but you still have six or seven sessions left. Let's see we can make more progress."

Ellie sighs. "I'll think about it, but I'm not sure I can handle any more disappointment."

"This might look different in a day or two. I'll give you a call in a couple days and see how you're feeling."

I hope that once the pressure is off, she'll reconsider. But, at this point, it might take a lot more than hope to motivate her.

Chapter Fifteen

Ellie

Ellie took her time after the session plodding back to her apartment on Arch Street. Not only was she a bit hungover from the medication, but she was sorely dejected by the failure to make any meaningful progress. She climbed the steps to her building and let herself in, but when she arrived at her apartment door, she could swear she heard music from inside. Since she couldn't remember turning on the CD player that morning, first confusion and then fear stopped her. What the heck was going on here?

Wondering if she should stay or leave, she gently turned the key to the lock and inched the door open without entering. If she had to run, she was in a better position in the hallway. To her surprise, she spied Damien with his feet on the coffee table, flipping through a magazine.

She pulled the door fully open. "What are you doing here?"

"Surprise," he said. "I wanted to be the first to learn about your session today."

"You actually took off from work to be here for me?" As shocked as she was pleased, she couldn't believe he'd take the time from his demanding job to be available when she most needed him. She immediately questioned her earlier opinion of him. Perhaps she had been too rash in her appraisal and he was someone she could depend on after all. Her heart swelled with tenderness and joy.

He rose and took her into his arms. "Come sit on the sofa and tell me what happened."

She could hardly believe he was being so loving and concerned. How could she have been so wrong about him? She let him lead her to a seat.

"So, how'd it go?"

She made a face. "Worse than I imagined. I regurgitated my entire life story up until the night Jessica's died, but I didn't recall a thing about that event. I'm as lost as ever...and a bit embarrassed to boot."

Sincere concern filled his eyes. "Too bad. I was hoping you would have a breakthrough of some sort. What a bummer."

He wrapped her in his arms and held her to his chest. The sudden show of support touched her so deeply, the tears she had been holding back flowed like a broken dam. He drew her closer and the warmth of his embrace offered her permission to release her pain and frustration. Only after he had gone into the bathroom to retrieve some tissues, did she pull herself together.

She wiped her eyes and blew her nose. "It's so disappointing."

"I can imagine." He took her hand in his and held it. Then his face lit. "How about we do something special for you?"

"What is that?"

"Lets go out for a bite to eat at that Italian Diner we always said we'd like to try."

She touched her damp face. "I must look a mess. I'm not ready for prime time."

He gave her a squeeze. "No rush. Take your time getting ready. It's still early."

The clock read 5:15.

All at once exhaustion overcame her. "I'll tell you what...give me an hour to rest and I'll get ready to go out."

"Take two. I'll watch the news while you nap."

She wandered into her bedroom and crawled into bed, but couldn't immediately fall asleep. Until that moment alone, it hadn't struck her how weird it was that he had let himself into her apartment without her permission. Even though he had a key, he had never entered without her prior knowledge. Under the circumstances, she couldn't be too upset. The fact that he left his job early to be with her and wanted to surprise her by being there when she arrived home, touched her. His consideration overshadowed any apprehension she might have about his taking liberties with her privacy so early in their relationship.

She wrapped the quilt around her, but even after quieting herself down, she had trouble dosing off. The fact that she might never retrieve memories of her last night with Jessica gnawed at her with the relentlessness of a starving animal.

She couldn't blame her problems on anyone or anything other than her drinking. It had left her vulnerable, an easy mark for whoever did Jessica in. Alcohol had ruined her life before, but it had never left her so clueless. If Jessica was murdered, catching the killer and protecting herself might be singularly dependent on her ability to remember the events of that fateful night. And it was looking less and less likely that would ever happen.

She vowed right then and there never, ever, ever to drink again. She had it with alcohol if it was causing her this much misery...and placing her at risk. She wouldn't take another drink if her life actually depended on it.

And she meant that with all her heart!

Reluctant to bother Jack again, but determined to reach him, Ellie dialed his number one more time. She had left him a few messages over the past month, but he didn't respond to any of them. Now, quite by surprise, he picked up on the third ring. "Hello."

Relief at hearing his voice flowed through her. At least she would no longer have to leave those annoying, long-winded messages meant to prompt a reply. "Where the hell have you been? Timbuktu?"

Jack chuckled. "Just busy. How are you?"

She didn't buy it. "I've been wondering if you've been avoiding me since my conversion to AA?"

"Nah. You're not as fun as you used to be, but I still love you."

"How about brunch on Sunday, then?"

Jack seemed to weigh the request. "Okay. Eleven at *Famous 4th Street Deli*?"

"You're on." She disconnected, but held her cell close to her chest. Did Jack's distancing himself had anything to do with Jessica's death? No matter what happened when they met, she planned to press the point. She couldn't go on much longer without knowing the truth.

Famous Deli was like most delicatessens in town. Bustling on Sunday morning with curt waiters and pushy patrons. Glaring florescent lights exposed a clean, clinical setting with black and white tiled walls and flooring. The glass counters near the entrance were loaded with meat, fish, salads and pastries. Behind the counters rye bread, Cholla, and bagels sat on shelves or in bins. In the adjacent room, tables overflowed with hungry families and lox specials. She stood in line waiting for both Jack and a table. Neither seemed to materialize for the longest time. Finally, the maitre d' led her to a table for two in the rear. No sooner had she taken a seat, than Jack raced in, face flushed.

"Sorry, I was held up in traffic."

She was about to admonish him for not leaving earlier, when she noticed his attire, a *Brooks Brothers* style cotton stripped shirt with khaki Dockers and brown loafers. The identical outfit to the man in her dreams. A chill ran through her and she rubbed her arms.

He took a seat across from her. "Cold?" he asked. "They should turn the air down. I'll let the waiter know when he comes by."

"I'll be okay. How are you? Long time no see," she said, attempting to make herself sound calm. "What have you been doing?"

Jack immediately picked up on the conversation and ran with it, rambling on about work and all the trips he had to take out of town. She only half listened, her mind stuck like an orbiting satellite, coming back time and time again to his clothing. It was quite a coincidence that he had dressed exactly like the man in the flashback. Was it possible that man could have been Jack? And what was he doing in Jessica's apartment the night of her death?

When he said, "Earth to Ellie," it broke through her reverie. "Where's your mind?"

She flapped a hand. "I'm so hungry, I can barely think."

Jack searched around and flagged a passing waiter who took their orders.

"So," she said, forcing herself to focus, "I know you've been busy, but it sure feels like you're intentionally steering clear of me. I've tried to call you a number of times and left messages, but you haven't bothered to return any of my calls."

Jack brushed his hand through the air as though brushing off her concern. "I'm sorry about that, it's just that I've been super busy with work and...I met someone new who I've been spending every free minute with. I didn't mean to blow you off, I haven't had the time."

While she doubted his authenticity, she knew Jack well enough to believe he might be easily distracted by a woman and readily abandon his other friends. She had seen him do this with Jessica. "All right, I'll accept your explanation. But why didn't you let me know sooner?"

"I was too embarrassed to tell you I met someone new only days after Jessica's memorial. It seemed so...I don't know...so disrespectful."

She made a face. "Why? You and Jessica broke it off awhile back. No one expected you to stay true to her."

His stare turned dark and mysterious. "She might have broken it off with me, but I never fully broke it off with her. In a strange way, I always believed we would eventually get back together. I never fell out of love with Jessica."

If he was being honest, how could he have moved on so quickly after Jessica's death?

"I wasn't sure how you and her other friends would take it."

"I can't speak for anyone else, but it doesn't bother me in the least. It's about time you found someone new. Jessica rejected you months ago."

He cringed. "I don't like thinking of it that way."

A tic appeared under his left eye. Was what he really didn't like thinking about the night Jessica died? Had he been there? And what part had he played in her demise? She glanced across the table at his striped shirt, and cringed, too. If he had played a part in Jessica's murder, was she sitting across the table from an innocent bystander, an accomplice...or the murderer himself?

Chapter Sixteen

Sarah

The room seems too cramped, the chair too hard, the conference table too long...and Aaron Davis too obnoxious. To admit my lack of success with Ellie's treatment is hard enough without having him rub it in.

"I hate to say it, Sarah, but I warned you this adventure of yours was unproven."

I try not to show my annoyance. "In this situation, it was worth a try. What did we have to lose that's not already lost?"

He wears an exasperated expression. "I'm not sure you should be experimenting with a patient. You could lose her and your credibility."

Sam lifts a hand. "What Sarah tried to accomplish was admirable." He beams me a warm and inviting smile that lights the dreary conference room. "She did everything she could in this situation. You can't fault her for that. It's too bad it didn't prove effective."

Cathy, who is always pleasant and agreeable, gives me a thumbs up. "You took a risk, Sarah, and even though it didn't work out as you hoped, it was a good thing to do."

Vindicated by all the backup, I am still far from satisfied. I had hoped to share a different outcome, but, atlas, it hadn't worked and Sarah hadn't returned for another session. "Well, I guess I've done all I can do here. I don't have anything else to share about today. I concede the floor."

"You sure?" Alice asks.

After I nod, she begins her spiel about an anorexic patient of hers and we spend the remainder of our staff meeting discussing this woman's case.

Sam calls an end to the meeting, I gather my files, but before I leave the room, Aaron approaches.

"I'm not trying to sabotage your case, Ellie, but I'm concerned about how you're using our time and resources."

I don't know how to respond. Time and resources. As the newest staffer, I have no desire to abuse the system. "I'm sorry if I'm using a disproportionate amount of your resources, but I was only doing what I could to help Ellie. This wasn't an attention grab, I sincerely wanted to be successful with this case."

"I understand, but there's nothing you can do to retrieve memory after a blackout. You're wasting our time. And, I, for one, resent that."

I hear the anger in his voice, but that doesn't mean I will succumb to his pressure. "It's probably too late to do anything for Ellie anyway since she hasn't called back for an appointment, but I will continue to do whatever I can to assist my clients. That's my job."

He looks relieved...excessively relieved considering what I had said. What's up with that? "Too bad she's gone, but I'm sure you'll be able to use your considerable skills with someone else." He gestures with his hands as he speaks, and I suddenly notice a substantial blue-stoned ring on his index finger. How did I miss it before?

Then I remember Ellie's description of the man in Jessica's room the night she died. According to Ellie, he had a ring on his index finger with a large blue stone. That sets off alarm bells in my head. Of course, lots of men wear rings on their index finger, but this was quite a coincidence. "I better go. I have an appointment at 2:00."

He follows me out the door and down the hall toward our offices and there, standing at the appointment desk, is Ellie.

I stop a few feet away from her. "Ellie?"

She turns and acknowledges me. "I was in the area and decided to stop by and make an appointment. Sorry I didn't do it sooner, but I needed time off after the last session."

Aaron comes to a halt beside me, a guarded look in his eyes. "Good to see you again, Ellinor."

Ellie smiles at him, but her gaze immediately descends to his hand and she stares open-mouthed at his finger. She quickly catches herself and looks back up at him. "Good seeing you, too."

"I better get back to work. Hope we meet again soon."

Aaron leaves us standing there mesmerized, watching him stride down the hall.

I snag Ellie's eye. "Nice ring, huh?

She looks as pale as an electro-shock patient after treatment. "Sure is. Hope he didn't notice me staring at it." The look in her eyes informs me she's thinking the same thing I am. "Not everyone has a stone that size."

"It's memorable, wouldn't you say?"

"Not one I would forget too soon." The expression on her face confirms her recognition.

And sends a well deserved sensation prickling my spine.

Later, as I am putting my paperwork in order before I leave the building, Sam sticks his head through my office door. "Busy, or can I come in?"

A strange sensation, almost like giddiness, fills me. "No, no, not busy. Come on in."

He takes a seat on the opposite side of the desk from me. "I wanted to apologize for the grief Aaron is giving you. He can be a tough customer, but I sense he's especially hard on you for some reason."

I am surprised and touched by Sam's awareness and concern. Psychiatrist are so often administrators and pill pushers, I didn't expect that level of humanity from him. "It has nothing to do with you."

"I know that, but you're all my staff and I don't like to see any of you being bullied."

At the realization he only considers me one of the staff, a smidgin of disappointment deflates me. "Don't worry about it, I have pretty thick skin."

"Even so, I'll talk to Aaron about what's going on. I'd like to nip this before it becomes a bigger issue."

"I'm not sure it will effect anyone else."

He makes a face. "What does that mean?"

"Only that it's a once in a lifetime situation. He seems most concerned about this particular case. I can't see that he'll react the same under other circumstances."

"I hope not, but you're still having to cope with his attacks. I want you to know that I'm here if you need my support."

Sam holds my eyes until, uncomfortable and feeling myself flush, I look away. "Thanks. I appreciate that."

He adjusts his wire rims. "What are you doing after this?"

"I was on my way home."

He glances at his watch. "If you can wait fifteen, I'd love to take you out for a drink. You deserve one after the hassle you've had with both Ellie's treatment plan and Aaron Davis." He stands. "Besides, since you're fairly new here, it's time we got to know one another." As he backs out the office door, he asks, "We on?"

I had planned on a quiet evening at home, but this sounds too good to refuse. "Okay. I'll wait for you here." With more than a bit of anticipation...maybe more than is warranted, but I can't seem to help myself. I finish filing folders and take a seat on my office sofa. It's been ages since a man has paid any attention to me...the last one almost killed me, but that's another story... and I'm more than flattered. I'm intrigued and enthusiastic, but I only pray I am reading his intention correctly because I would hate to be disappointed again.

Chapter Seventeen

Ellie

After leaving the Wednesday night AA meeting in South Philly, Ellie slid into her *Hyundai Accent* for the ride home. Although she sometimes walked to the meeting, it was located in a marginal area and she preferred to drive over after dark. Once in the car, she noticed the overhead light had been left on since before the meeting when she needed to locate her cell phone. Worried, she tried the ignition, but the engine failed to start. After a couple more attempts, she left the vehicle in search of help. Fortunately, Hank was opening his truck door as she wandered by.

"I hate to bother you, but my car won't start. Is there anyway you help me out?"

"Sure," Hank said. "What the problem?"

"I ran the battery down and I could use a charge."

Hank went around to the back of his truck and pulled a pair of jumper cables. "We're in business. Where's your car?"

She pointed him to her Accent and he backed his truck out of the space and pulled up alongside her car. He helped her hook up the cables. She slipped back into the car, turned the ignition and it started without a hitch.

"Thanks," she called out to him. "Can I give you a few bucks?"

"Nah. I'm sure I'll ask you for a favor someday." He detached the cables and approached her car door. "I'm glad it'll get you home, but you better take it into a shop tomorrow to make sure it has enough juice. I hope you don't need a new one."

"That would be a bummer, but it's not all bad because, if it hadn't discharged, I wouldn't have run into you tonight. How've you been doing?"

"Happy, joyous and free. Better off than that boyfriend of yours."

"Why? What's wrong with him?" she asked, even though she wasn't sure she wanted to know the answer.

"I don't know. He seems to belly ache about work a lot lately."

"Yeah, I've heard it too." Although hesitant to ask the question on her mind, she might as well while she had Hank's ear. "Has he said anything about me?"

Hank gave her a small smile that could be interpreted as nasty or nice. "Just that you've been working through some relationship issues."

Her hands clenched the wheel. "Did he mention what those 'relationship problems' were?"

"Something about his having to work long hours."

"That's true. Anything else?"

"Besides the fact that he loves you and wants to make it work, only that he was worried about you. Seems like you've been struggling a lot lately."

Hearing from Damien's sponsor that he still cared for her brightened her day. Her hands relaxed. "Really? Sometimes he doesn't appear to be too concerned about me."

"You're all wrong about that. He's into you." Another biker type materialized by Hank's side and they began to converse, giving her an excuse to take off. "I gotta go. Thanks for the help.

She stepped on the accelerator and pulled out of the parking spot, her mood buoyant after talking to Hank, more hopeful and happy than she had been in a long time. Perhaps everything would work out with Damien after all.

She pulled to the curb in front of her building and almost skipped back to her apartment, energized by Hank's encouragement. Immediately on entering, though, she sensed something was wrong and her balloon deflated. At first she wasn't sure what it could be, but she quickly realized the magazine she had purposely left open on the coffee table that morning, so she could finish reading an article on problem relationships, had been folded shut. Someone had been in the apartment while she was out and the only person who had a key aside from her and the superintendent, was Damien. But what would he have been doing there? And if it wasn't Damien, who could it be? A bolt of fear raced through her.

She fished around in her purse for her cell and gave Damien a call to clear her mind.

He answered on the third ring. "Hi Babes. What'sup?

"Were you at my apartment today?" she asked.

"No, why?"

"Someone was."

She heard a laugh.

"You have to be kidding. I'm too busy to leave work right now. It's been one hell of a day. The new programmer quit so I'm having to do his job and mine. The last thing I have time to do is to visit you. As a matter of fact, I might be working late again tonight."

Even though she wasn't especially surprised, she could really use his company after discovering the intrusion. She hated herself for being such a cling-on. Why couldn't she grow a backbone? "No problem. I must have miscalculated where I put things."

"You're on edge so often lately. Maybe it's because of that failed session with your therapist, but you're overreacting to things. Have you thought about dropping out of therapy?

"Not really..."

"Maybe you should. Why don't you go get one of those frozen custards you love? It might make you feel better."

Anything would make her feel better than she did at this moment. It was after nine and Damien was still at work.

When she failed to answer, Damien asked, "Are you still on the line?"

Barely. She drew a deep breath and steeled herself in preparation of what she was about to say. "And since you're working late, why don't we skip tonight and get together tomorrow?" While she dreaded the idea of not seeing him, she prided herself on not appearing as needy as usual.

She must have surprised him because there was a hesitation on the line. "Okay...if that's what you want."

"It's not necessarily what I want, but I have to go in early tomorrow and I want to get some sleep."

"All right," he said. "I'll see if I can get away earlier tomorrow night. Either way I'll let you know."

She placed the phone on the table and slumped back onto the sofa. While pleased with how she handled Damien, it meant being alone all night even though she still had the eerie sense someone had been snooping about her apartment. Someone other than Damien.

For a tall woman, she was a timid, frightened sort.

Still lost in thought the following afternoon, Ellie took an alternative route home from work. While the walk was intended to take her mind off of Damien and what had occurred at her apartment the night before, that's all she could think about. Distracted, she was surprised when she found herself at 19th and Market, across the street from Damien's office.

While she knew it wouldn't sit well with Damien's boss if she pestered him at work, she stared up at his fifth story window hoping there might be a chance of spotting him. But all she could make out were shadows moving around behind the vertical blinds.

It wasn't long before she questioned her own sanity for remaining outside his building and turned up the street at a good clip, running smack into Jack.

Jack grabbed her arm to stop her. "What the hell are you doing here? Isn't this a bit out of your way?"

Even though innocent of any wrong-doing, she felt as though she'd been caught in the act. "I had an appointment with my gynecologist today. Can't a girl get any privacy in this town?"

"Not in Filthydelhphia," he joked. "Hey, since you're here, how about a drink?"

"Nah, I think I better get home. I have a lot to do this evening."

Jack tightened his grip on her arm in a commanding way and steered her forward. "I want company. Come on. I know of a joint around the corner. I'll buy you a water."

The pressure on her arm and the way he tugged her along made it clear she had little choice. This wasn't a request, it was a demand. "Ouch, you're hurting me."

Instead of responding, he continued to hull her forward to a dive about a block and a half from his building. Inside the place was as sleazy and small as it appeared on the outside, but dark enough to hide most of the damage. He shoved her into a booth at the back and shouted to the bartender an order for a beer and two waters. He held a hand clamped to her arm until they were served. "Now tell me the truth. Why you were outside my office today."

She raised both hands in front of her face. "I didn't even know where your office was until now."

"It's quite a coincidence that I find you right outside my building. Come on. You think I was born yesterday? What's going on?"

Why the suspiciousness? Did he have something to hide? "To tell you the truth, my boyfriend works in a building across the street from yours. I came to visit him, not you."

He downed his beer and asked for another, his gaze never wavering from her face. "I've had the distinct sense of you shadowing me ever since I told you about my feelings for Jessica. And today you've confirmed that perception."

She raised her hands. "All you professional types have offices downtown. How did I know you worked in such close proximity to Damien?"

"Why are you constantly hounding me? It's all too weird."

"If you mean the calls, we're friends, aren't we? I wanted to keep in contact with you."

"We were both Jessica's friends, that's our only connection. I don't know what you want from me or why you won't leave me alone, but I'm not your man."

"My man? What do you mean by that?"

"I mean you're barking up the wrong tree if you believe I had anything to do with Jessica's death. I'm not the person you should be tailing."

Why was he protesting so much? "Who then?"

"How the hell do I know. All I know is it isn't me. So look elsewhere."

She stood, hoping he wouldn't prevent her from leaving. "Okay. I promise to stay out of your way." She broke for the door before he had a chance to follow.

Once outside, she quickly blended into the crowd on the sidewalk and weaved her way as far as she could before she needed to stop and take a breath. The anxiety in the pit of her stomach had grown into a spasming chasm. Not only had someone been in her apartment the night before, but she had been man-handled into a dark corner of the city and intimidated into silence. The more she looked into Jessica's death, the more murky and frightening the picture became. And it had yet to fully reveal itself.

Things were appearing darker by the day. Even though she was afraid to look any deeper, she felt compelled to do so. No longer a wish or a whim, it might be the only thing that could save her life.

Chapter Eighteen

After a lovely evening with Sam, including drinks and dinner, I wish him goodnight at the restaurant. He tries to convince me to let him walk me home, but I remain adamant I can take care of myself. I cut through a parking lot and follow a short cut back to Queen Village.

I had only gone a couple blocks, when an uneasy sense of eyes on me takes me by surprise. I scan the street, but there are so many people milling about, it's hard to distinguish who might be tailing me. To secure a better vantage point, I step into a corner market and duck behind a rack of magazines by the window.

A man with a baseball cap and sunglasses meanders past, but even though it's unusual to wear shades this late in the day, he appears distracted and pays no attention to the store. Others are also preoccupied or rushed. No one enters the facility.

Sequestered where I am, I attract the attention of the cashier who might have thought I was casing the joint. I quickly pull myself together and go on my way, but the sense of being followed has vanished. Either I had been daydreaming, or my stalker had noticed my maneuver and decided not to become the stalked.

Checking behind me one more time, I make a mad dash in the direction of my condo townhouse, rush inside and slam the door behind me, throwing the deadbolt with a decided click. I lean back against the door and cover my racing heart with a hand. This intimidation has to stop. I can't go on this way. Is it Drew following me, or am I merely imagining it? I lift the receiver and phone the police station. It's time to allow the detectives to do their job.

Later, after speaking with a couple of officers and seeing them on their way, I mix myself a stiff drink to calm my nerves. The police promised to drive by my home and office on a more regular basis, but beyond that, there was nothing they could do until I had an authentic encounter with Drew, or whoever else might be harassing me.

Funny, Ellie also complained about a feeling of being followed, without being able to prove it or not. And she also suspected someone had been in her apartment when she was out. It reeked of similarity and was too coincidental not to be connected. Could it be the same guy? But who could have a stake in both of us...besides...Aaron. I banish that course of speculation because I can't see the relevance in my case.

If it's Drew, I can understand why he'd be after me, but why her? I have to discover if he's the one behind my sense of violation and vulnerability, or if I've conjured up this entire scenario out of fear that he's back in my life? The only reason he would return is to locate Rachel. Otherwise, why would I still be on his radar screen?

I flick on the television, but nothing appeals to me besides the news, which is centered on a missing woman, offering me no peace. Instead, I crawl into bed with a good book, hoping only to be safe and sleep soundly. I promise myself not to let anyone frighten me, or find Rachel. I will do everything in my power to protect us both.

In the morning at the weekly staff meeting, I rub my tired red eyes and drink an extra cup of coffee to keep myself awake. Twice I find my eyes drifting closed while listening to Aaron drone on about a kleptomaniac patient, and, the second time around, he shoots me a dirty look. It's unprofessional to behave this way, but I'm powerless to control it.

When it comes time for me to present my case, I gulp the coffee and sit upright to keep myself alert. I clear my throat. "In terms of Ellie's progress, she's back in treatment after taking a couple of weeks off, but we're stuck at a standstill. I'm totally at a loss about the next step. Since chemotherapy didn't work, I'm not sure if there's another therapeutic tool I can use with her that might be more effective. I might be forced to discharge Ellie unless we can find another treatment."

Aaron shrugs. Cathy makes an exaggeratedly sad face. Alice avoids my eyes. This case has become a sticking point for the entire staff.

Sam shakes a finger at me. "I have an idea."

The entire table, except Aaron, leans forward.

"And what is that?" I inquire.

"This past weekend I read an article in one of my neurological journals about a phenomenon they labeled State Dependent Memory. Wait," he jumped to his feet. "I might still have a copy in my office."

Sam bolts the room and, minutes later, rushes back in brandishing a wrinkled magazine. "Here it is. Let me see." He flicks through the pages. "Okay, let me read this to you. 'Early anecdotal evidence suggested that blackouts might actually reflect state–dependent information storage—that is, people might be able to remember events that occurred while they were intoxicated if they returned to that state.' That was written by D. W. Goodwin and some of his colleagues in 1969."

"That's ancient history," Aaron says. "Why bring it in now?"

"Because, as late as 2002 another researcher, White, along with his colleagues found evidence that confirmed these findings. And, the article goes on to point out that there are many instances where drinkers have stashed money or keys only to locate them again once they're intoxicated."

Suddenly I'm not so sleepy. "So, you're saying it might be possible if Ellie drank again she could fill in more details of what happened the night of Jessica's death."

"It's a long-shot," Sam says, "but might be our only hope of helping her."

Aaron vehemently shakes his head. "It would be highly unethical to ask an alcoholic patient to drink. You could lose your license for that one."

"You don't have to worry about that, because she's already told me she will never drink again no matter the circumstances. I can't believe she'd choose to do that even if it's her only way out of this mess."

All eyes remain glued to me. "I don't even know if I'd have the heart to suggest it after all she's gone through to gain sobriety. It will create intense conflict for her."

Sam hands the journal to me. "You should at least look this article over and do your own homework before you make any decision on how to proceed...or not. Let me know what you're thinking once you've done your research. Now let's move on to the next patient. Alice, it's your turn."

While Alice shares, I can think of nothing but Ellie. I can't say I'm thrilled with the solution Sam, but what if it were her only option? What if it meant life or death for her?

I glance over at Aaron knowing I can't include him in the decision-making process and expect an unbiased or supportive position. He might toss a grenade in the works by threatening to report us to the licensing board.

Then I look over at Sam and my pulse quickens ever so slightly. Even with his thinning hair and sharp features, he holds a certain spell over me. In addition to being my boss and my confident, I know he's on my side and would do anything in his power to help me. And that knowledge alone endears me to him.

Sam stops me in the hallway as I leave the office the following afternoon.

"Going to lunch?" he asks. "Because I'd like to tag along."

"So happens I'm on my way to the soup and salad joint around the corner. You game?"

His lips curl in the sweetest grin which lights up his face. "I have to complete one last task. Land us a table and I'll be there in ten."

More like fifteen or twenty minutes later Sam races through the door, looking more disheveled than normal. "Sorry, I had to take a call on the way out. You know, one of our funding sources." He plops into the seat catty-corner to mine.

"No problem. I ordered. I'll signal the waitress that you're here."

He places a hand over mine. "I'll take care of it." He waves at the waitress from across the room. She detours to our table on her way to the kitchen and takes his order.

He turns to me. "I was thinking about that article and the momentous decision you have to make. I know you must be terribly conflicted about what to do, but I want you to know there's someone you can run things by."

"Aaron," I say with a chuckle.

He makes a face at me.

I smile. "Thanks. That's considerate of you. It's all I've been able to think about since I left the meeting yesterday."

"I can imagine."

The waitress places my salad plate on the table and assures Sam his sandwich is on the way.

"Asking Ellie to drink again must go against every fiber of your being."

"No doubt."

"But it might be the only tool left in the toolbox."

"How can you even be certain it works? I read the article. Many neurologists question the efficacy of the procedure. How can I ask her to forsake her sobriety for something as iffy as this?"

The waitress places a BLT in front of him, but he ignores it in favor of addressing me. "Of course, you're right, I would have the same ambivalence you do. I know it must be eating at you."

"It's driving me crazy. I'd suggest it to her in a heartbeat if I considered it a legitimate and effective option, but I'm not sure. I have to let this idea percolate before I can make a good decision. I'm hoping time will offer me more clarity."

He unfurled his napkin. "I'll be available anytime you wish to process it with me."

I stop eating, my fork in mid-air. "As much as I hate being sneaky, I think it would be smart not to mention this to Aaron. He's not only antagonistic toward it, but who knows how he'll try to sabotage our work." I put my fork down. "I discovered that Aaron had a relationship with Ellie's deceased friend at one time."

Sam sits back, looking stunned. "Seriously?"

I nod.

"Why didn't you mention that to me before? It might be a conflict of interest to even have him consulting on this case."

"I would have said something earlier, but I only learned about it well into the consultation. Had I known, I would have asked him to excuse himself from the case."

Sam still looks shocked. "Well, that shines a new light on things. Do you think his antagonism toward you might have anything to do with this past relationship?"

"Could be. And he might have a personal investment in the outcome of this case."

Sam raises a brow. "What kind of personal investment?"

"I don't know for sure, but it seems from his reaction to everything I try to do with Ellie, he might not want me to succeed. Ellie's friend, Jessica, broke off the relationship months before she died, but there's still reason to believe he still had an investment in her. His attachment might be getting in the way of his supporting my goals with Ellie...or his motivation might even be worse."

"Worse?"

"Ellie dreamt she saw a man standing by Jessica's bed on the night she died. In the dream, he wore a school ring with a large blue stone." I let that sink in. "Aaron wore an identical ring last week. There's a possibility he was in Jessica's room that night."

Sam places his napkin on the table and sits back. "That's a lot to take in all at once. I'm not sure what I should do about all this."

I reach out and cover his arm with my hand. He watches me, warily. "We don't know anything for certain, so I don't want to alert Aaron to the fact that we're suspicious of him. I want to play it cool for awhile until we have more information. Don't do anything just yet." Suddenly uncomfortable with the intimacy, I remove my hand. "But I'd like to keep Aaron out of our treatment plan. I don't want him to interfere."

Sam stares down at the place on his arm where my hand used to be. "All right. I'll keep things cool for now, but I'll have to monitor the situation and make sure we're not stepping over any ethical or legal lines. I promise, I won't do anything without your knowledge. I hope you'll do the same for me."

"Okay, boss, I'm in." I grin, grateful to have Sam as my co-conspirator and my support system. I wouldn't want to do this alone, without someone having my back, and it's especially pleasing that Sam will be the one I can turn to if the going gets rough.

Chapter Nineteen

Ellie

Ellie withdrew more and more from her meetings and social life because, no matter where she turned, fear and a sense of vulnerability followed her. Her awareness that someone had her on his hit list seemed to grow with every passing day, even though nothing in reality had changed. She was in danger...and she knew it. While Damien tried to be supportive, he wasn't around enough to offer her what she needed.

For the third time in a week she faced another night alone. Damien had been working long days and was no longer around on a regular basis, which tormented her no end. Although exhausted, after a busy afternoon working on a complicated immigration case, she didn't want to spend hours alone in the apartment, fretting the hours away. She tried calling Damien, but reached his voicemail. Next, she thought about Jack, but realized she couldn't call him after their last encounter. Without Jessica around, she had no close woman friends to call on and, since her parents and brother had moved to Florida, her only local relative was a distant cousin. She tried her sponsor, but again, no answer.

For the first time in weeks she considered finding a Happy Hour, but besides the initial excitement, the thought unnerved her. She had better do something to take her mind off drinking. Instead of heading home after work, she took the elevated train downtown. Macy's was open late and she would busy herself shopping for a new outfit. Even though she didn't have the money to splurge on clothing, it had to be better than splurging on booze.

An hour and a hundred and thirty dollars later, she left Macy's and wandered the downtown streets trying to lose herself in the crowd. She walked a couple of blocks and ducked into a small Chinese restaurant she had frequented in the past. The owners, an older Chinese couple, were always gracious and the food tasty. Although she had been trying to lose a few, she munched on spareribs and Shrimp in Lobster sauce. No use holding back. The meal had no more calories than a handful of drinks and offered the opportunity to quiet the raging storm inside of her.

Dusk had descended by the time she landed back on the street. Behind the buildings, reds and golds lit the early nighttime sky. She trotted in the direction of the El, but before she reached the station fear paralyzed her for no apparent reason. She could hardly catch her breath. Again she heard Jessica calling her name. Goosebumps sprung up on her arm. She forced herself to walk another block, but could go no further. She slipped into a convenience store.

After picking up a Snickers bar, she studied the street through the picture window. She immediately spotted a man in what appeared to be a black hoodie half-hidden behind a pole across the street from the store. Even though she couldn't see his face with a dark colored hoodie over his head, from the position of his body, he was facing her. Still frozen to the spot, she plucked her cell from her purse, googled Uber and called a driver. Within five minutes, a car pulled over to the curb. She crept out of the store, even though the stranger was no longer there, sidled into the backseat, making herself as inconspicuous as possible. She gave the driver her address then watched as the car passed skyscrapers and street lights, then row homes and parks on the way back to her apartment.

As she passed a corner bar, she had the strongest urge to ask the driver to pull over. Instead, she scrabbled around in her purse, searching for the fortune cookie she hadn't eaten. When she opened it, the fortune read: *You are in for a Big Surprise soon*. What kind of surprise? She'd had her share of surprises lately, she didn't need anymore. Peace and serenity was what AA had promised her. But where was this peace and serenity? And would she ever find it?

The Uber driver dropped her off in front of her apartment building. She raced up the steps to the building, let herself in at the same time a neighbor approached the door. Feeling safer, she chatted with this neighbor for a few minutes, before gathering up her mail and making her way upstairs.

In the apartment, she placed the mail on a table by the front door, when she heard a noise behind her. She was about to turn around when someone ran into her, knocking her over with such force, she smacked her head on the coffee table and crumpled to the floor. Although stunned, she looked up in time to glimpse a man in a black hoodie stealing out the door.

Wounded and shaken, she curled into a ball, hugging her legs to her torso. It took her a good five minutes before she could pull herself together enough to sit up. Her head ached fiercely and the room spun. It took another minute or two before the spinning slowed. Finally, she forced herself to rise, locked the door, and checked out the damage.

First, herself. She glanced in bathroom mirror and noticed a raised red lump swelling beneath the skin on her forehead. She unsteadily made her way into the kitchen where she put together an icepack to stop it from enlarging any more.

Next, she surveyed the apartment for anything missing, but nothing in the living room looked out of place. In the bedroom her laptop had been lit with an eerie glow. Since she had shut it down before leaving in the morning, seeing it turned on took her breath away. She grasped her arms over her chest before she approached the computer...then gasped. The hooded intruder had been reading her email.

This invasion of privacy was too overwhelming to bear. Her head still spun from the fall and she could barely put two thoughts together. With wobbly legs, she lowered herself to the edge of the bed trying her damnedest to make sense out of what had happened, but nothing computed. For at least fifteen minutes the blanket of confusion and shock made it impossible to consider the possibilities.

Finally, the fog lifted and she was faced with the facts: A man had broken into her apartment, not to harm her...although her head throbbed like crazy...or steal anything of value, but simply to read her emails. In a way, this seemed more dastardly than stealing her mother's diamond ring or her new flat screen tv. And it caused her far greater anxiety. This wasn't a random case of burglary. This was a planned attempt to lift information about her off her computer. The realization shook her to the marrow.

She wrestled the phone from her purse and called the police, who arrived thirty minutes later. The two officers who took her statement were gentlemanly enough, but didn't hold out much hope for an arrest, especially since nothing had been stolen or destroyed.

After they left, she brewed a cup of Camomile tea and took a seat on the sofa. The break-in had left her drained, both physically and emotionally, but even in her depleted state, she knew it was a turning point. Whoever the stranger was, he was out to get the goods on her. She felt the noose tightening, her life was in serious danger. She could no longer be laissez faire or take her time learning about what happened to Jessica. She had to know the truth, no matter what she had to do to discover it.

Her time was running out.

Chapter Twenty

Sarah

"So, the last time I saw Ellie, something had changed," I tell Sam, leaning forward with elbows on his desk. "She's determined to learn who's trailing her and said she would do whatever it takes."

Sam nibbles the tip of his pen. "How does that effect your decision?"

"I'm still not sure what to do, but I'm reconsidering."

"Okay, but you have to keep in mind the consequences of her using alcohol."

I roll my eyes.

"I know it's obvious and I sound redundant, but as your boss, I have to say something. So, tell me more about what happened that has you reconsidering all this."

"Okay," I said. "Here's how it went ..."

Ellie described the incident with the intruder, hands peaked in a gesture that was more pleading than pious. Lines formed on her forehead and around her mouth as she spoke. The office seemed so still you could almost hear the tissue I unsuccessfully handed her sail to the floor. 'I hate this. I haven't been able to sleep since the break in.' Tears leaked from her eyes and driveled down her cheeks.

'I hate that you're having to go through this.' I handed her a fresh tissue.

'And what's worse, I'm scared to death he'll be back again...and for me this time.'

I debated whether to suggest the alcohol therapy to her. Already in a tough dilemma, I hated to place her in another one, but would I be able to live with myself if something terrible happened to her and I could have given her a way out? 'What if I could offer you a option for dealing with this, one that might compromise your recovery, but might lead to a real breakthrough? Would you want to learn about it?'

Her face lit up with an expression of hope. 'Of course.'

I expected that response, but I didn't know if I was prepared to tell her the only way out of one trap was to enter another. 'It's a problematic and not necessarily proven one.'

'Sounds more and more tempting. What's holding you back?'

'I'm afraid the option I'm about to suggest might mean all that you've done the last few months will be compromised.'

She watched me with a serious but expectant expression. 'Are you saying I might have to drink again?'

'That's exactly what I'm saying. If you want to recall the night in question, the only other idea I have is for you is to drink under clinical conditions.'

'Oh." She sat back and exhaled loudly. 'That's a surprise coming from you.'

'I know, but it might be our last remaining tool. There's some experts in my field who believe you can overcome blackout amnesia by recreating the state in which the memory was imprinted on the central nervous system in the first place. But there are others who debunk that theory as impossible and unrealistic. So, there's no guarantee it will work, but I have nothing else I can offer you.'

Ellie stared at me. 'So, let me get this straight. If I drink again in the hospital under medical supervision–'

'And hypnosis,' I added.

'And hypnosis...I may or may not be able to recover the events of that night. Right?'

'Right.'

'So, I'd have to sacrifice my sobriety for a possible, but not necessarily sure-fire solution.'

When she said it that way, I went a bit queasy. 'Right.'

She covered her mouth with a hand. 'I promised myself I would never, ever, ever drink again and you're suggesting I do it for therapeutic purposes. Right?'

I nod.

'I'll have to consider this. To be honest, as frightened as I am, I'd be willing to do almost anything, except...drink. To lose my sobriety, and then have this not work...well, that would be devastating. I don't know...'

'In the best case scenario you'll be able to remember what went on the night in question, and you won't have any compulsion to continue drinking after the session, but there's no guarantee on either score. One option that might help ensure you don't end up relapsing is to place you in an alcohol treatment program immediately after the session to solidify your sobriety, but that's as far as I've taken this.'

'I was able to stop drinking before, but this time with a maniac on my tracks, who knows what I'll do.'

'Granted. And I would only want you to do what felt safe for you. I don't want to influence you either way. The only reason I brought it up is because it's the only solution that's presented itself to me lately. Since your life might be at risk, I had to share it.'

She wiped her eyes and tossed the tissue. 'Because this whole incident with the intruder has thrown me for a loop, I'll give it some serious thought before I see you again. But I have to tell you...I've been toying with the idea of moving away from Philly and starting over again...you know, like in that witness protection program, with a new identity and all. But that would be damn hard to do. Still drinking again, and risking everything I've gained lately, might not be any easier. I don't want to lose the little bit of recovery I have, but I also don't want to lose my life.' She rose as though the session was done, although my watch told me there were ten minutes left.

'I'm overwhelmed right now, but I'll mull it over and get back with you next session.'

I walked her to the door. 'In the meantime call if you need any clarification or to discuss this further.'

'I will,' she said, and gave me a quick hug.

I watched her shuffle out the doorway, seeming a bit stunned, then turned and leaned against the jamb. I had given Ellie an almost impossible puzzle to solve, and she would have to put all the pieces together herself. As much as I wished I had the blueprint to keep her safe, that was beyond me and my competence.

While I speak, Sam pushes his chair away from his desk and extends his legs, listening intently. When I conclude, he sits upright and maneuvers his chair to the desk. "Interesting therapeutic relationship. It sounds like you are both coping with similar conflicts around this drinking issue. It shows how powerful a bond you have with your client."

"It also shows the extent of the threat Ellie is experiencing, both from this psychopath on the loose as well as from the booze. She has a difficult choice to make and there's no right and wrong decision. I wish I could make it easier for her, but I can't."

"And, that would be inappropriate. As much as you're connected to Ellie as a patient, it's not your place to tell her what to do, to make things simplier for her, or control her actions. You know that."

"Of course, I do. But that doesn't make it any easier to heap this much responsibility on her shoulders at a time when she's so vulnerable."

"What choice do you have? Except, maybe, joining me for a bite to eat after this."

I know he means this as a way to console me, but it's the last thing I want to do. All I can think about is spending my evening with my sister and Dicky. Being around my active, curious nephew always takes my mind off my problems. "Sorry, I have plans with my family this evening. Can I take a rain check?"

Although Sam smiles, I can see the disappointment in his eyes. "I'm glad you aren't going to be alone. We'll do it another night." And while he sounds brave, he quickly shows me to the door. "I still have tons of work to do before I leave. Have fun with your family."

"I will. Goodnight." Before I know it, I am on the other side of his closed door, wondering about his sensitivity. But I had bigger worries and they quickly replace my concern about him before I even make it back to my office.

I sit across the dinner table from Lara. "I need to run something by you."

"I'm all ears," Lara says. "Except for the mouth that's about to yell at my son. Wait a sec."

Dicky had been running back and forth across the dining room the last couple of minutes. Lara looks totally distressed. "Dicky. Dicky, do you hear me? I'm about to put you in bed if you don't quiet down. I'm trying to listen to your Aunt Sarah and you're making it impossible. Now you either play a video game or it's bedtime for you."

"Aw, Mom. I'm bored." Dicky pulls at Lara's arm.

Lara rises, takes his arm and walks him over to the computer. "I know, sweetie, but I need to speak with Aunt Sarah. As soon as we're done, you and I can read from *Lord of the Rings*. Okay?"

Dicky jumps up and down. "Yeah!"

"Now play a game while I talk to Sarah and I'll come and get you when we're finished."

Much to my surprise, Dicky does as she asks and boots up the system. He's certainly beginning to mature.

Guilt-ridden for disrupting Lara's time with her son, I ask, "Is this a bad time for you?"

She snorts. "Is there a good one when you have an eight year old at home and your hubby is working late? I don't think so. Go on."

"Okay, but feel free to break in if you need to..."

"I won't."

I clear my throat and ponder how to present my dilemma without giving anything confidential away. "I'm wondering as a professional what you would do in a certain situation." Even though Sarah hasn't worked in the field since Dicky's birth, she has a degree in social work, years of experience and a license posted on her home office wall, which is fortunate for me.

"Lay it on me."

Disguising Ellie's name, I tell Lara about her alcohol problem and the potential treatment. Lara listens attentively. I explain my conflict then ask Lara if she has any advice. Silence follows.

"That's a tough one. I wish I knew what to tell you, but I never came across anything like it when I was working in the field."

"I don't mean to put you on the spot, but I don't know where else to turn for advice. I hoped you would be able to give me your opinion or, at least, point me in the right direction."

Lara pats my knee. "I wish I could be more helpful, sis, but since going on leave, I'm not equipped to give you that kind of advice. Why I can hardly manage my son or balance my checkbook any longer. I'd hate to steer you in the wrong direction." She pours me a fresh cup of decaf. "All I can tell you is that I'd be careful with liability and all. I'd hate for you get yourself into hot water."

Of course she's right. If something happened to Ellie, I'd be the one responsible.

"Aren't you surrounded by other professionals," she asks. "Seems like you have a built in support system. That's where you should turn with this."

To whom? I had already run this by Sam and, while he was supportive, he didn't have any answers and he ushered me to the door. There's no way I would share it with Aaron and I don't know the social workers well enough to trust they'd be of any help. Addiction medicine is so specialized. You need a background or training in it.

I chide myself for putting Lara on the spot. Sure, she attended Al Anon for awhile because of Will's pot use, but that doesn't make her an addictions' expert. While I'd love validation that I'm doing the right thing, it isn't fair to bring Lara into this. The idea I could find affirmation outside my own gut instincts is delusional. Anything I might do...or not do...could end disastrously. No one had the reassurance I sought...or the answers.

"You're right, I shouldn't have bothered you with this. What I need is expert advice. Now, tell me more about how Dicky's doing at day camp."

While I make an effort to listen to Lara's description of Dicky's shenanigans, my mind wanders repeatedly back to Ellie. Only time, and the outcome of her therapy, will put this unsettled feeling to rest.

And there's no guarantee even that will work.

Chapter Twenty-One

Ellie

After her workout at the gym, Ellie grabbed a sandwich at a nearby deli and headed home. Damien had promised her he'd take off from work earlier than usual and meet her for a cup of tea and a talk. She had to process her choices and come to a decision, because she hadn't been able to focus on anything else all day. Her boss had noticed her mental absence and questioned what was going on. What was Ellie to tell him? *I'm about to relapse in the name of therapy.* How well would that go over at the office?

She let herself into her darkened apartment with a racing heart. Ever since the break-in, she tensed every time she opened the door, half expecting someone to be inside. She quickly switched on the light and scanned the main room. Seeing it was empty, she surreptitiously made her way to the bedroom and bath. With a huge sigh of relief, she released her clenched fists. It was safe this time, but how about the next?

As she placed water on to boil, she thought about what she was going to tell Damien. While intrigued with the idea of being intoxicated again, it also petrified her. Part of her salivated at the thought, while another part recoiled as she would from a hot flame. She had been scorched more than once by alcohol, she didn't want to be burnt again. Her heart raced with anticipation...and dread. She had promised herself she would never drink again. Would she actually consider breaking that promise?

The kettle whistled at the same moment there was a knock on the door. She let Damien in with a hug before turning the burner off. "What perfect timing. I'll brew the tea."

She put some loose peppermint tea in the caddy, lowered it into the pot and poured the boiling water over it, carrying the pot and mugs into the living room where Damien had taken a seat on the sofa. She placed the pot on the coffee table and sat down next to him. "How was your day?"

"Okay," he said with a shrug. "At least it was shorter than normal. That's the best I can say for it."

"Why? What happened."

"My manager is on my case again about productivity. Seems I can't do enough to please her. But I didn't leave early to talk about me. What's going on with you?"

Ellie smirked. "Early? It's already 7:30. Early is 5:30."

"Okay." He looked annoyed. "Earlier than I normally do."

"I have a bit of a dilemma and I wanted to run it by you." She poured the steaming brown liquid into their cups.

Damien reached for his. "What situation?"

Ellie blew on her mug and took a short sip of blistering tea. She placed it on the table to cool. "Sarah's found a way to help me recall what happened the night of Jessica's death."

"That doesn't sound like much of a dilemma. It sounds like the answer to your problems."

"It's the procedure that's the catch."

"And that is?"

Ellie fortified herself. "I would have to drink again."

Damien choked on his tea. "What? Did I hear you correctly?"

"From your reaction, I'd say you did."

"Why the hell would you need to drink? It's seems counterintuitive."

"There are Psychologists who believe you can retrieve a blacked out memory if you recreate the state you were in when you blanked out."

Damien shook his head violently. "No. No. No. You're an alcoholic. If you drink, you could lose your sobriety. Who knows if you'll ever get it back again. I'm totally opposed to your doing this. As a fellow addict, I can't sit back and watch you sacrifice your sobriety for some dumb-ass theory."

"But, what other choice do I have? Nothing else seems to be working."

He rose. Towered over her. "You have a choice all right. You have a choice to stay sober and not do anything foolish in the name of therapy. I forbid you from doing this crazy thing."

How dare he talk to her that way. She had never seen him so irate and unreasonable. She respected his concern for her recovery, but, for once, she wasn't about to let anyone, even Damien, boss her around. She stood and faced off with him. "I need your support, not your intimidation. Your bullying me isn't helpful at all."

"It's just that I'm worried about you."

"I understand, but even if I do take the plunge, I'll be doing it under clinical supervision, and they plan to place me in rehab for a few days after the treatment. I'm not certain what I want to do either. That's why I wanted your unbiased opinion."

"I told you my opinion. I'm totally against it. You'd be nuts to take the risk."

"But if I do decide to do it, can I depend on you?"

"You're putting me in a horrible bind. I don't want to fail you, but I'm absolutely opposed to your attempting this. I don't want to give you any indication that I'll back you up."

"It would destroy me if I couldn't depend on you when I needed you most."

He wore a rigid, sullen mask. "I'll do what I can, but there's no way I will do it cheerfully."

"All right. If that's the best you can do, I'll have to live with it." No use hammering home the issue any longer, she knew where he stood and it wasn't necessarily with her. If she decided it was the right thing to do, she might have to do it on her own without his acknowledgement and backing. A stiff breeze of fear and resentment passed over her. "Now lets drink that tea before it goes cold." But not nearly as cold as she felt.

The next day offered no more solace for Ellie. While the attorney she worked under was out of town, he had left her with a brief to type, calls to make and filing to finish. Too busy to focus on much else, the day slipped by. Finally, on the bus ride back to North Philly, she could think of little other than her predicament.

Going over the possible outcomes time and time again with no resolution or direction was driving her crazy. She needed a less biased friend to bounce it off of. Ordinarily, Jessica would have been that friend, but now Ellie needed someone else. But whom? Her sponsor had been out of town visiting an old friend for the last couple of days and she didn't want to disturb her, but she needed another opinion.

Then she remembered Damien's sponsor, Hank. She had bumped into Hank at a couple of meetings lately and was always impressed with his friendliness and generosity of spirit. The last time she saw him she had mentioned a problem with the garbage disposal and he offered to fix it. He had given her his cell number. She looked for it in her contacts and dialed the number.

On the second ring, Hank answered. "What can I do for you?"

"I was wondering if you had any time to fix my pesky garbage disposal?"

"No prob." They made arrangements for him to come by the following evening at six.

At exactly 6 P. M. the next day, the doorbell rang. Ellie let Hank in and they exchanged greetings before she showed him into the kitchen. He immediately went over to the garbage disposal and tested it out. The piercing noise it emitted made her cringe, but that didn't stop him from shoving her broom handle into the device. After a couple of shoves, the melody changed to a more sonorous grinding sound, far less jarring on her nerves.

He flicked it on and off a couple more times. "I think I got it."

She thanked him with a lemon lime soda in the living room. Hank finished his off, before leaning forward, elbows on thighs.

"So, what's going on with you?"

"Nothing special, except that I have to make a decision about whether to drink or not."

He laughed, but then seeing she was serious, whistled through his teeth. "I wouldn't call that 'nothing'. That's momentous."

"Yeah...you're right. I just can't decide what to do."

Hank wore a quizzical expression. "What's to decide? Seems like you'd either do it or not."

So, she explained her dilemma to Hank.

Hank listened closely with a frown plastered on his face. "So what does Damien say?"

"He's not exactly enthusiastic about the idea, but why should he be? He has to live with the outcome."

"I'm with Damien all the way on this one. The last thing you need to do is start drinking again. You'd be throwing away too much...and for what? A hope and a prayer about learning the truth. A long shot. I wouldn't advise it."

Strike two.

All at once she realized how much she had been hoping for a different outcome...for someone...anyone...to corroborate her choice. Until that moment, she hadn't realized she wasn't asking an opinion, she was seeking affirmation. She had already made up her mind.

Normally, she would never make a decision of this magnitude without the backing of others because she didn't trust her own instincts. She had a long-standing pattern of going from one person to another looking for validation and this behavior was becoming painfully obvious in light of her present actions. "I have to do something..."

"Anything you do out of fear and neediness is insane and will not end well. You know the definition of insanity: Doing the same thing and expecting different results. I wouldn't do it if I were you."

Wasn't that exactly what she'd been doing by balloting numerous people, looking for somebody to give her the answer she wanted to hear in the first place? But would she have the nerve to undertake the treatment in the face of discouragement and opposition? "Okay, that seems to be the consensus so far. I only have one more person to run it by."

"Who's that?"

"My sponsor."

"That's a waste of time because what's she gonna say that's different from Damien and me?"

He probably was right. Surprised by the depth of her disappointment, she remembered what they taught her in AA; that she had no control over people, places, and things. If her sponsor, Maddy, concurred with the others, she would certainly listen...but, for once, she would make up her own mind. She was tired of letting other people's opinions rule her life. It was time to stand up for herself. "You could be right, but she's my sponsor and I need to run it by her when she's back in town tomorrow."

The next morning, Ellie rang Maddy and was relieved when she answered on the third ring. Thank goodness Maddy knew so much about her situation she didn't have to repeat her story another time.

After she had gone into some detail about her choices, Maddie asked, "So, what's the problem?"

"This therapy is unproven. I would hate to lose my sobriety and have the procedure reveal nothing. It would be heartbreaking."

"But wouldn't it be equally heartbreaking if you didn't try it and never had a chance to figure out what happened to you? Wouldn't you always regret not doing this when you could?"

At that moment, she wished she could reach through the telephone line and throw her arms around Maddy. She had been waiting for someone to say those exact words. As frightened as she was of the after effects of the alcohol, deep down what she wanted was to do the therapy. Having her sponsor's support solidified the decision she'd already made. "Thank you. I needed that."

Maddy chuckled. "Sure. No problem. I'll be there to help you with your program when you're ready to return. And you have all of your AA sisters behind you and what sounds like a terrific therapist. I wouldn't hesitate if I were you."

And, with that seal of approval, she wouldn't either.

Chapter Twenty-Two

Sarah

"I received a call from Ellie today and she set an appointment for later this afternoon to discuss how she wants to proceed," I tell Sam. "I'm a little nervous about meeting with her, because I'm still not sure about the right thing to do, but I know the real decision is hers."

Pushing back from his stately cherry wood desk, Sam slouches in the overstuffed black leather office chair. His eyes barely betray his anxiety over Ellie's decision, but I can read the tension in the set of his mouth. He interlocks his fingers and twirls his thumbs as he listens to me.

Whatever Ellie decides, it will not only effect her, but all of us on the mental health unit who work with her. By doing alcohol-induced treatment, we are straining the legal and ethical limits of therapy and nobody does that with impunity and ease.

"Is there anything you'd like me to take care of if she agrees to the regimen?"

"Make sure you have all the correct documents signed before we go forward. I'll check with our lawyer about writing an agreement, waiver, and any other forms we'll need before we proceed."

I stand. "Okay." My legs shake ever so subtly. As difficult as this is for the hospital, the final onus is on me. If anything goes wrong, I will take the fall. But I'm compelled to do what is in Ellie's best interest. I can only hope and pray the drinking doesn't lead to a full-blown relapse. I'd never be able to live with myself if it did...and I might even lose my license to practice."

Sam's eyes soften as though he senses what I'm thinking. He rises from his seat, moves to my side, and places an arm around my shoulders. "Don't worry Abrams. I'll stand by you whatever happens."

"Unless you have to defend the hospital against me. Where will you stand then?"

He places two fingers under my chin and tilts my face toward his. "Lets cross that bridge when we come to it, but I will do my best to be there for you every step of the way."

The look in his eyes, at first tender, mutates into something deeper and more dangerous. I start to look away, but, before I do, he lowers his lips to mine in a kiss both sweet and sensual at the same time. Desire rushes through me and for a timeless moment, I revel in the sensation.

Remembering where I am, I pull back. "I wasn't expecting that."

"Neither was I, but I've been dreaming about it ever since I first laid eyes on you."

I force myself to look away. "I meet with Ellie at 4 o'clock today."

"Can we do a drink after your session? I'd like to know how it goes."

Even though a part of me wishes to escape to the safety of my condo, I remain stuck in the gravitational grip of that kiss and have no power to decline. "Okay. I'll meet you at *32 Degrees* at six if you can get away."

"I wouldn't miss it for the world," he says in a throaty voice that mimics my own. A bolt of passion pulsates through me. "See you there."

After a powerful and emotional hour with Ellie, I leave the clinic for a walk to unwind and process the session. I have forty-five minutes before my meeting with Sam, but I need to take time for myself and breathe the late afternoon air. I trudge along 7th Street to Washington Square and take a seat on a bench under a large Maple tree. I often take lunch breaks in the park, admiring its greenery in the midst of the concrete and steel jungle. The pastoral quality quiets my nerves and replenishes me. I need to surround myself with living vegetation after a long morning of listening to stories of suffering. The park has become that place of peace and solace in my world.

As much as I had hoped Ellie would choose the treatment, I quake at the notion of what might happen. That woman has more chutzpah than she realizes. The fact that she's willing to challenge her disease in order to discover the truth fills me with hope and humility, but I can't help but feel the fear beneath the tenderness. What if she can't stop drinking this time? There aren't any guarantees, no matter how often she has recovered in the past, she'll be able to do it again.

Even though it's a warm late summer eve, I wrap my arms around myself for comfort. That I might be instrumental in instigating a full-blown relapse, scares the hell out of me. No matter how much sense it makes to attempt this last ditch therapy, the outcome could be disastrous and, for that, I will be the one to blame. Even if Sam and the crew forgive me, I will never be able to forgive myself.

I glance around and spot someone slip behind a Maple not far from me. When they fail to reemerge on the opposite side, goosebumps rise up on my arms. Again, I have the unmistakable impression I'm being followed. I've put up with enough of this invasion of my privacy and the subsequent intimidation. Instead of slithering away, as I would normally do, I spring from my seat before I have a chance to reconsider, and stride toward the mature tree. I haven't gone more than half the distance when a young man, of about seventeen or eighteen, steps out from behind the tree and walks away. I look around and spot a young girl not far from here, sprawled out on a blanket. Most likely the object of his attention.

I watch him leave the park and disappear into the crowd rushing by on 7th Street, then return to my place on the park bench. Have I become that much of a paranoid maniac that I am chasing teenagers and shadows in an attempt to protect myself? Have I totally lost my grasp on reality? And will I ever be able to trust my own perception again?

All I know is that I'm in trouble. I have to find a way to take charge of my mind...before it does damage to me.

At *32 Degrees,* I make my way to a seat at the end of a black table surrounded by red upholstered chairs and order a glass of Chardonnay. Sam has yet to arrive, but this gives me a chance to appreciate the well appointed club. Chic and sophisticated, it shimmers with recessed lights. Bottles glisten from behind the long black bar. Music pulsates from a surround sound system. Everywhere I look well dressed professional types sip on colorful drinks and nibble on tempting hor d'ourves. With its exciting and romantic vibe, this isn't an appropriate place to discuss business.

The waitress arrives and Sam rushes up behind her. "Sorry I'm late. I had an important call right before I left the office and I had to take it."

"No problem. I'm enjoying my people watching."

He claims a seat caddy-corner to mine and orders before the waitress can run off. Then he smiles at me. "I'm so glad you could meet me outside the office. I needed to get away."

I sip my wine. "Me too. It was an intense afternoon."

"I can't say mine was any less stimulating." A gleam lights his eyes and reminds me of our kiss. "So, how was the session?"

I gulp the wine this time. "She wants to try the therapy."

"Not surprising, I guess. How are you doing under pressure?"

"A bit jittery. A bit hopeful. You can never be fully prepared for this type of thing. I mean, we're experimenting with more than her psyche...we're experimenting with her life. It's a lot of responsibility."

He encloses my hand in his and holds it for a minute until the waitress arrives with his drink. Then he releases it in favor of a long swig of beer. "It is, but if anyone can handle the consequences, it's you. You're an experienced, empathic, and outstanding psychotherapist. I'd trust you with anyone."

I'm both flattered and flustered. I'm not certain how to respond to his effusive compliments because I don't want to disappoint him. "Thank you, but I'm not sure I can live up to your adjectives."

"Then live up to your objectives. You only have to do your best. That's all anyone can expect of you...even Ellie."

"I hope so..."

He chugs down his beer. "I need to speak to you about something."

I clutch my hands under the table. What can it be that makes him sound so darn serious? "Are you all right?"

He stares at the table and my blood pressure skyrockets. "I don't know how to say this... it's just that I really, really like you, Sarah..."

Uh oh, here it comes.

"But after our kiss today, I had to clarify my situation for you—"

"You're married!" I blurt out.

Again, the downward glance. "Yes..."

"Oh God..." Both horrified and embarrassed, I spring to my feet and am about to exit the bar, when he grabs ahold of my arm. "Don't go. Please hear me out."

I stand by the table, primed to flee but unable to move.

"Please sit."

Reluctant at first, I finally reclaim my seat. "Okay. What do you have to say for yourself."

"You're right about my being married. I've been married for twenty-seven years, but a few years ago my wife developed something called Huntington's Disease."

"Oh no." I know a bit about this disease. "That's terrible."

"Her deterioration has been heartbreaking. My wife was a spunky independent woman, but with this disease, she's lost her ability to do so many things that we take for granted. She's wheelchair bound, has no real short-term memory and has to be fed and groomed. I can't tell you how miserable this has been. Even though there's a woman in that chair, for all intent and purposes, I've lost my wife."

This time I reach for his hand. "I'm so sorry. What a horrible thing to go through. I had no idea..."

"Of course, you didn't. I don't mention it to most people because I don't want their pity or their advice."

"I get that. You won't hear either from me."

"Good." He smiles glumly, his gaze as distant and full of sorrow as my most depressed patient. "After the kiss today, I knew I had to tell you because it wasn't fair to keep you in the dark about this. I hope you will forgive me for my attraction to you and my wanting to be with you. I can't help myself." He turns his sad eyes on me. "But I would understand, knowing what you now know, if you don't feel the same way about me."

I'm quiet for a moment. "What I know is that you're a fabulous man. No matter what happens between us, I admire you for being there for your wife, and for being honest with me."

"Does that mean I stand a chance?" The hope in his eyes nearly breaks my heart.

As much as I want to make it right by him, I have to take care of myself. "I admit, you're a man who often exceeds my expectations and I admire you tremendously..."

"But?"

"But, since I wasn't prepared for this revelation today, I'm going to have to give it some serious thought. I'm sure you understand."

"Of course, I do, but I hope you'll forgive me. I didn't expect it to go this far."

I beam my love onto him. "Forgive you? I'm extremely flattered. How could I have anything but gratitude?"

"Thank you for your compassion."

"It's more than that," I said. "Don't forget I'm depending on you to help me with Ellie. I can't do this therapy without your medical expertise."

"We're still a team, Dr. Abrams?"

I raise my palm and he slaps it with his. "We are unbeatable, Dr. Roseburg. And don't you ever forget it."

With all the arrangements completed at the hospital, I gather up my files to leave for the day when Aaron comes rushing into the office, curly hair ruffled and eyes wild. "What the hell is going on here? I've heard you've arranged for a procedure room on Friday afternoon. What is this all about?"

So, Aaron has an insider in administration backing him up. "Yes, I did. Why? Is there a problem?"

Aaron runs a hand through his unwieldy hair. "The only reason you would need a room is to do the unsubstantiated and unethical treatment you mentioned. That's why."

Caught in the act. There's no use denying the truth. It will eventually become known. "It's the only option we have left for Ellie. We have nothing else to offer her."

"Huh," Aaron said loudly, "And you believe this treatment is safe and effective. How about if it backfires on you and doesn't work? Aren't you giving her false hope. This could be a real bust."

My stomach spasms. "Don't you think I take this seriously? I'm as anxious about it as anyone. But right now, Ellie wants to do it and I'm obligated to give her the chance."

Aaron's eyes narrow. "I'm not going to let you get away with this, Sarah. It's unprofessional where I'm concerned. If you attempt to do this procedure with Ellie, I will report you to the Board."

As upset as I am, I hold his gaze, but his is unwavering. "I hope you don't report me because I'm only doing this out of a firm belief it's in my patient's best interest, but I guess you'll have to do whatever you believe is best."

Red in the face, Aaron looks like he's about to pop a blood vessel. "Too bad that you've already made up your mind, Sarah, but it's not too late to change it. If you don't, you won't hear anything more from me, but expect to hear from the authorities."

He looks as if he's about to strike me. Quaking inside, I refuse to show it. I raise my head and place my hands on my hips. Finally, he storms out of the room and down the hall. I slouch back against the wall, hand over my chest.

Aaron seems determined to stop me by any means available. What's his stake in preventing this procedure? And will he really act out on his threat?

I'm not sure I want to know the answers in advance.

Chapter Twenty-Three

Friday couldn't arrive soon enough now that Ellie had made the decision to proceed with the alcohol therapy...all her hopes pinned on discovering what happened to Jessica. It could be her only way of figuring out who was stalking her and avoiding a catastrophe.

But even more than that, a shiver of excitement at the idea of being tipsy again tingled through her. She wished she didn't feel this way, but it only confirmed what she already suspected...she was a full blown alcoholic. No one else would experience anything other than dread, knowing how alcohol had affected her in the past.

She placed the book she had been reading on the bed because she had reread the last paragraph three time and it still didn't compute, her mind preoccupied with the next day. Since the session was in the afternoon, she had chosen to take the morning to herself. That way she would have time to prepare for what was to follow. No one could tell her for a fact what the outcome of the treatment would be, but she was banking on it to shine a light onto her present situation. Even though she had a handyman add an extra lock on her front door, ever since the break-in, she had lived every moment in terror. Only the knowledge of who might be after her would put her at ease. Desperate, she wanted to put an end to her stress.

Even if she did recall, would that be the end of it? Sure, she would recognize the face of the demon, but wasn't that the reason he was on her tail? Once he knew she did, what would he do? Perhaps her awareness would only embolden him...and not protect her. But this was a risk she had to take.

She rose from her bed and reached for her desk drawer to consult her morning schedule. If she had nothing major planned, she would spend it at the gym, working off at least part of her anxiety and anticipation. She opened the top drawer and immediately noticed the schedule book wasn't in its usual place. Had she moved it? After pushing aside pens, paperclips and staples, she found it shoved in the back of the drawer. This stopped her. In the habit of placing the book in its appointed place, she couldn't imagine she would sequester it in the rear of the draw. The earlier shiver had become a shake.

Again she was reminded that someone had been in her bedroom and gone through her things. It was more than her computer he was after. She thumbed through the book, hoping to notice something awry around the time of the break-in, but it wasn't until she came to the most recent entry that she noticed a crinkle in the page. The idea a stranger might have been leafing through her information didn't sit well with her.

Whoever had been in her apartment had apparently returned. But how did they get in? Only one person beside herself and her landlord had access to her premises...Damien, but it didn't make sense that he would be there when she was out...hell, it was hard enough to get him over when she was there. Of course, he had been over the night before last. Perhaps he had gone through her drawer when she was cooking. He could have been looking for a pen or paper. Anything was possible.

Or her landlord might have let someone in to figure out the problem with her stove burner, which she had been complaining about for months, or change the battery on her smoke alarm, but why hadn't she been informed in advance? If he had allowed a worker entry to her apartment without her knowledge, it was a major breach of her lease.

With all this in mind, she could barely catch her breath. She placed her hand over her heart which was galloping along at an incredible pace. Damn, this was unsettling.

Take a breath, she had to remind herself. Taking a seat on the bed, she inhaled and exhaled a number of times until she could sense breath slowing, her body softening. Enough was enough. She couldn't handle much more of this harassment. She could only hope that the next day would bring relief from this misery. If it didn't...she didn't want to consider what she might have to do because that thought scared the hell out of her.

Fortunately, Sarah didn't leave Ellie waiting in the lounge too long, because she was unable to pay attention to anything other than the entryway in anticipation of the session. She tried to concentrate on the magazine in her lap, but any sound, even the click of the clock, demanded her attention, and she'd find herself staring one more time at the infernal doorway. When Sarah finally strode through it, Ellie sprang to her feet before being summoned.

Ellie followed Sarah into the same room where she'd been treated with the truth serum. An examination table filled much of the room, surrounded by a metal tray table, an intravenous pump and, what had been described to her in the earlier session as heart and saturation monitors. After removing her shirt, donning a cotton robe and positioning herself on the table, Sarah's co-conspirator, who Ellie knew as Dr. Roseburg from that earlier truth serum session, greeted her and prepped her for the therapy by taking her temperature and blood pressure before attaching the monitors. She prayed that this session would be more fruitful than her last foray into experimental treatment.

"I'm going to insert the IV," Roseburg said, before inserting the needle into the back of her hand.

She flinched at the sting.

"Okay?" he asked.

She nodded. "What should I expect?"

"I'm about to turn on the saline solution. Once that's going, I'll add alcohol to it, gradually increasing the amount until it becomes obvious you are mildly intoxicated. I will continue to monitor your condition while Sarah plies her magic with you. My job is merely medical. Sarah is your therapist."

He faded into the background, fixated on the instruments. Sarah pulled a chair alongside the table. "How are you doing?"

"Normal...well, as normal as can be under the circumstances."

"Dr. Roseburg hasn't started the alcohol yet, but you'll know when he does. Let me know what you experience as this progresses."

Sarah glanced over at Roseburg and Ellie followed her gaze. When he nodded, she knew the show was about to being. "Okay...I'll do that."

Sarah repeatedly checked in with her, but nothing changed for a minute or two. Then she began to feel an elusive, but familiar, warmth slither up my spine and flow outward toward my limbs. "Whoa..." She closed her eyes, savoring the sensation of relaxation and pleasure that coursed through her veins. Her arms loosened at her sides, her breathing slowed to a more normal pace and her eyes drifted shut. "I'm beginning to feel it..." Her thoughts slowed until they were in sync with the rhythm of the IV drip. Words thickened, became viscous in her mouth, then her mouth slackened and she sensed herself drool. "I'm gettin' drunk..."

Behind her, Roseburg toyed with the instruments. "I'm shutting this down some."

She was woozy, but still aware. "I'm allllrighttt." She could hear the slur in her words, but no matter what Ellie did she couldn't make them come out straight. "Don't ja worry 'bout me."

Sarah lifted a brow. "Okay. It's time to do our work. Close your eyes and take a couple of deep breaths through your nose, hold for a few seconds and release them through your mouth."

She tried to do what was suggested, but each time she inhaled she coughed out the air. Finally, after a couple more tries, she held her breath and released it.

"Now, I want you to return in your mind to the evening of your last Happy Hour with Jessica and describe to me moment by moment what you experience."

For a few minutes nothing happened. She tried to conjure up the events of that night, but all she could see was floaters and hazy images. Even the part she remembered seemed to fade and distort.

Unable to concentrate for long, she drifted off.

Suddenly the scene changed.

"I...I'm seeing something...wait..it's becoming clearer...it looks like I'm arriving at the nightclub where I'm supposed to meet Jessica in the sleek black suit I had worn to work that Friday. Jessica's already at the bar and I take the empty stool next to hers...she's ordered a vodka martini and I order the same as a way to celebrate her recent raise.

Thirsty, I down the first couple of drinks, only taking a pause for a quick bathroom break...ooolala...the third drink has arrived by the time I climb back onto the stool...um...the alcohol and excitement of the evening has me in its grip. Jack is busy chatting with Jessica on my far side so I turn to the neighbor on my right...he's an older man, with graying hair, but he seems glad to have the company...he buys me a drink and I finish that one, too. When I turn back to Jessica, Jack's no longer at her side...she's talking to another man, who I overhear order us both drinks...the drink materializes in front of me and I sip on it, promising myself I will take it slower this time around, but it seems to disappear more quickly than I anticipate...after complaining, Ralph on the right buys me one more.

By this time I'm woozy and ready to leave...I turn back to find Jessica in a spirited discussion with the man on her left and have to tug at her arm to get her attention...Jessica looks over at me...she's inebriated, slurring her words...her mascara has etched a black line down one cheek.

Sarah's voice broke through the fog. "Did you catch a look at Jessica's companion?"

"I dunno.,,I can't remember..."

"Look over at him now. Tell me who you see."

Ellie's mind wandered and she had to stop and force herself to look over at the man seated by Jessica. *She gasped. "Shit!"*

"Who do you see?"

"I can't believe this...what a fool I've been."

"Who is it, Ellie? Tell me who it is." Sarah touched her arm. "Is it Damien who you're seeing?"

Elle had begun to cry so hard she had trouble catching her breath to answer. *"Why? Why? Why? I don't understand...why is he doing this to me? Why has he befriended me? I'm so lost..."*

"Let's not assume anything. Who is it, Ellie?"

"Damien's sponsor...Hank. It's him. No wonder Hank wanted to know so much about my therapy...he's been stalking me in so many ways..even referred me to you."

"Interesting." Sarah was quiet for a minute as though she was taking it all in. "What happened next?"

"We had another drink...Jessica said it was getting late and she wanted to continue the party at her apartment...I can't remember the ride there, but, next thing I know, I'm in Jessica's kitchen and Hank's handing me a mixed drink. I take into the living room and plop into a chair.

"And?"

I dunno...I must have passed out...suddenly I'm awake...there's a loud quarrel in the bedroom...I look over...Hank's standing at the end of the bed... Jessica's yelling at him that she remembers where she knows him from and she knows what he's done..she threatens to call the police if he so much as touches her.

He tells her she has that all wrong and reaches for her...but she continues yelling at him...he grabs her by the shoulders and shakes her...she's screaming obscenities at him, but the more she screams, the harder he agitates her...in the midst of her yelling she calls him a lowlife...he turns bright red in the face, his rage palpable even from a distance...oh my God...he grabs her around the waist...she calls to me; Ellie, Ellie, but before I can rise, he hauls her above his head and smashes her to the ground...I try to scream, but panic stifles the sound...what's he doing...oh, no, he's stooping down beside her...oh, God...he's raising her shoulders and thrusting her head into the metal file cabinet in the corner...Damn...I hear a loud sound, like a crack. Everything goes silent.

In shock, I try to stand, to go over to Jessica and help her out, but before I can, I'm knocked back down and stumble into my chair where I must have passed out again...I dunno how much time went by, but the next thing I hear is a loud groan and I pry open my eyes to see Aaron at the foot of the bed...tears are dribbling down his cheeks...he keeps mumbling, Jessica, Jessica, Oh no, Jessica...over and over....I don't remember what happened...maybe they had one of their fights...I ignore him in favor of a drink to quench my thirst. I pass out again."

Overcome with remorse, Ellie wrapped her arms around herself and sobbed. Sarah slung an arm over her shoulders and told Roseburg to turn off the juice. Even though she had accomplished what she wanted to, and there was no more reason for her to drink, Ellie hated the idea of coming back to reality after what she had learned. She turned on her side away from Sarah, too consumed with guilt for not doing enough to help Jessica to accept any comfort. She brought her knees to her chest, hugged her legs, and continued to cry until long after the alcohol wore off. Sarah stayed by her side until the tears dried and all that was left behind was an empty feeling in a lonely place...her life.

Later that day, Sarah personally drove Ellie over to her new group home. No longer drunk, she was light-headed, as if she'd been doing somersaults all day, and her mouth was as dry as a martini. Slightly nauseous, she was relieved when they finally reached the well-appointed, sprawling Colonial in Germantown with the landscaped yard of red, yellow and orange roses mixed among chrysanthemums and Lilies.

Sarah had to help her from the car and up the steps where a slightly disheveled, sixty-something woman greeted them.

The woman held out a hand. "I'm Olivia. I own this joint. Come on in and make yourself at home." She held open the door and they entered a large parlor with high ceilings and a huge stone fireplace.

While Ellie hoped it wouldn't be her 'home' for long, she was grateful to have a cozy and safe place to spend a few days after her ordeal and immediately collapsed onto a tufted, Victorian style sofa with floral upholstery.

"You must be exhausted after today. Why don't you rest a few minutes while I have Sarah fill out some paperwork. Afterwards, I'll show you to your room."

Ellie gave Sarah her insurance card and laid her head back against the sofa. Next thing she knew, Olivia gently tugged at her sleeve.

"I hate to bother you, but this place will fill with everyone returning from a meeting in a few minutes. Why don't I take you to your room so you can catch a good snooze. Later, when you're rested, I'll introduce you to the other patients."

Patients? She didn't see herself as a patient. Feeling more impatient for sleep at the moment, she rose, but before following Olivia up the stairs, she gave Sarah a farewell hug. "What's next?"

"Go get some rest. I'm leaving you in good hands. We have plenty of time next week to discuss how we're going to proceed." With a salute, Sarah left for her office.

Ellie turned back to Olivia, who took by the hand and led her to a room with a brass bed and burl wood dresser.

"You're going to like it here."

She said this with such conviction, Ellie almost believed her, although she knew this was only a temporary break from a starring role in the next act of her upcoming life drama.

Chapter Twenty-Four

Sarah

After another long day, I clear my desk and load my briefcase to leave the office. Lara had called to invite me for dinner and I accepted, grateful not to have to cook, or more likely, purchase fast-food on my way home.

As I place the final folder away, Sam pokes his head through the doorway. "Have a moment?"

"Sure. What's going on?"

He offers me a solemn stare. "Aaron. That's what."

"Oh, yeah. Is he still on the warpath?"

Sam enters the office. "He stopped by to complain about you, but I intervened by telling him what we had learned from Ellie."

"And..."

"It got a reaction out of him. He immediately began to defend himself, swearing he didn't have anything to do with Jessica's death, but came upon her later...after she was already dead."

"Why was he there to begin with?"

"Says he stopped by to convince her to see him again. Claims he's still in love with her and would never do anything to hurt her. All he wanted was to prove his sincerity to her."

I don't know whether to believe Aaron or not. "So why arrive so late?"

"I asked him that exact question and he claims that he knew Jessica was going to Happy Hour. He said he timed it to be there when she normally returned. He went into a long spiel about how this might look, but she was already dead when he arrived." Sam shakes his head. "I'm not sure what to do with all this. Whether to fire him or not."

I rise and walk to the end of my desk where I take a seat on the corner nearest to him. "Yeah, that's a tough one. His statement seems to correlate with Ellie's memory of events, but who knows."

"I wish we could know for a fact what happened that night, but all we have is a statement from a drunk woman. Seems iffy."

"I don't think this testimony will hold up in court. I called the police and have an appointment tomorrow to give my statement, but I assume they'll question its authenticity. I mean, first Ellie doesn't recall a thing and then we have to feed her alcohol to help her remember. Seems the DA could punch all kinda holes in that one."

"What do you think they'll do?" Sam asks.

"Probably question Ellie, but that might be as far as it goes. We might be on our own with this one."

Sam's eyes open wide. "What do you mean on our own? I'd say we're out of luck without police support."

He stares at me as though waiting for my concurrence, but I hesitate. I have no intention of letting this matter drop even if the police fail to do their job. Without a clue about how to help Ellie, who is at extreme risk with a killer on the loose...a killer she can now identify, I frown. "Of course, you're right. But, hopefully, we'll figure out a way to convince the police to protect Ellie. That's my main concern."

"Naturally." He lowers himself to the desktop next to me. "You're a damn good therapist, Sarah, and don't you ever forget it."

"Don't you ever forget it."

He catches my eye. "How can I? Have you had a chance to consider what you want to do? You know, about us?"

Had I considered much else? "I'm sorry, but with this Ellie issue, I haven't had time to focus on anything else. Once this is resolved, I'll be in a position to give it more thought."

"Okay, but please don't leave me hanging indefinitely. It's too hard to work with you day in and day out without knowing where I stand."

My turn to be solemn. "You got it boss. I promise."

He rises and trudges out of the room, looking more burdened than I had ever seen him. Even though I can't honestly give him an answer yet, I ache for him and a large part of me wants to call after him, but it isn't fair or right to say anything until I make a firm decision...one I can stand by forever.

Later, after a satisfying dinner of vegan lasagna and salad, Lara puts Dicky to bed and returns to the table with two cups of steaming decaf. "Jeez, am I bushed. You'd think I do something more in a day than shop, cook, clean and chase my son around the house to protect him, the cat, and all things perishable."

"That sounds like a lot to me. All I do is sit around and listen to people's problems. I'm the one who should be entertaining you." I send Lara a smirk so she'd know I didn't mean what I said.

"Good idea."

I follow up with another smirk. "Yeah, right. When do I have the time. Maybe next weekend. I'll let you know."

Lara flaps her wrist. "That's okay. I was only joking."

"Well, I wasn't. I'd love to have you guys over. It's been forever. And anyway, I'm going to owe you one after this evening."

Lara eyes me suspiciously. "And why would you owe me?"

"I'm afraid I need more advice from Dr. Lara." I clear off the table and return with chocolate chip cookies I picked up at my favorite bakery. An obsequious gesture, since I know how tired she is, but I need to throw myself on her mercy.

She sips the coffee. "All right. What is it this time?"

"Man troubles again."

Lara studies me. "I'm not sure I'm the one you should be coming to with your man problems. I almost got you killed last time I gave you advice."

I had relied on Lara to give me direction with Drew and that turned out to be a near-death experience. She lifts a conspiratorial brow, knowing we're both thinking the same thing. "I don't have anyone else to turn to but you."

Lara sighs. "That's a fine mess you've gotten yourself into." She sighs again. "Okay, what is it?"

I proceed to tell her how much I like and admire Sam. When I mention, as nonchalantly as possible, that he's married, she interrupts me. "That's unacceptable. I don't care what a great guy he is."

I let her have a couple minutes to rant and rave before I intercede with an explanation about the situation with his wife. Lara sits back, a hand over her heart. "Oh my, that is a complication."

Grateful she listened well enough to acknowledge the depth of my dilemma, I continue. "I'm not sure what I should, or even what I want, to do."

Quiet, Lara looks like she's deep in contemplation. "It's interesting for someone as quick to react and as opinionated as I am to be without an answer, but I'm at a loss here."

"Me, too."

"Maybe we had both better sleep on this one and address it again when I come over for dinner this weekend."

I smile at her willingness to be there for me when I need her the most. What a blessing she is in my life. "I promise vegan, but I can't promise it will be edible." And I leave it at that.

Discharged from alcohol rehab the next day, Ellie calls to say she's taking a detour by her apartment to refresh, but she still makes it to our session on time. She looks well considering her recent ordeal, but the moment she opens her mouth, tears flow.

"I'm at a total loss. The police took my statement, but it looks like all they're willing to do is question Hank. They told me they need more solid evidence before they can take any action. Matter of fact, my eye-witness report didn't impress them at all. And since I don't know Hank's last name or anything about him except his phone number, which has been disconnected, questioning him might not be in the cards unless they can track him down."

Not surprised, I ask, "In the meantime, what can we do to protect you?"

"We?" A guffaw. "It seems that I'm on my own again. What can *we* do?"

I ignore her cynicism "We can begin with my offering you the key to a friend's house. I know this is a bit unusual, but my friend is out of town for a few more months and has offered to let you use her house as a safe house for now." I hand her the key.

Ellie's eyes well with tears. "You'd do that for me?"

"Of course. It wouldn't be right allowing you to stay in a life threatening situation after what we've discovered. That's the least I can do."

Ellie stares at the key with open-mouth. "Thanks, Sarah. I don't know what I'd do without you."

"No problem. I want to be of help."

She looks sheepish. "I'm sorry if I'm being difficult. It's just that I'm scared to death."

"Understandable." I hand her a tissue. "Since you won't be able to stay at Cynthia's indefinitely, we"ll need a plan."

"What do you have in mind?"

I consider. "Maybe the next step is to find out all we can about this Hank fellow. Do you know anything about him at all?"

"Nothing more than I've already shared, but Damien might know more. I'm going to meet him for dessert this evening. I can pick his brains."

I place my legal pad on the table. "Good. Do you know if the police are looking into the phone number you gave them? Since he had to have paid for service, perhaps that will lead somewhere."

"Unfortunately, it was one of those burner phones."

"Is there anyway to trace the calls?"

"Don't know. They didn't mention anything."

"Okay, can you follow up with them and see if the calls reveal anything?"

She nods. "I don't know what they'll be willing to tell me, but I'll try."

I stand. "Okay, until we have more information, I want you to lay low. I don't want Hank to know anything about where you're staying, or have anyway of getting to you. Why don't you wait for me this weekend to return to your apartment and retrieve what you'll need to move into Cynthia's house. Don't go back there alone."

"Okay, I can do that."

"Whatever you do, remember, you are in a highly charged, dangerous situation. Please take care of yourself and be safe."

Ellie hugs me before leaving, but hesitates at the door. "I've never felt like I mattered that much to anyone, Sarah, but I sense that I matter to you. I appreciate your kindness and will do my best to deserve it."

As soon as she's gone, I slouch into my chair, calling on whatever force exists in the universe to protect her against all damage, deception...and peril.

On my way to the staff meeting the following day, I turn a corner in the corridor and run smack into Aaron. He barks out an apology before raising his eyes and realizing it's me. Startled, he stutters, "I'mmmm, ah, I don't know, I mean..."

The look in his coffee brown eyes is one of unadulterated fear.

I almost feel sorry for him. "You don't have to be self-conscious around me. I know you were in Jessica's apartment the night she died, but I don't have any reason to believe you were the one who killed her."

Aaron paled. "I didn't hurt her, Sarah...I swear to you it wasn't me..."

"Don't worry," I reassure him. "We have another person in our sights." A look of relief washes over his features. "But I do have one question for you. What were you doing in Jessica's apartment that night?"

His face falls. "This is so uncomfortable, I don't know how to tell you, but...I had to talk with her that night. I wanted to let her know how much I loved her. To convince her to give me a second chance. I loved her, Sarah. The last thing I would have done is threaten her. It isn't in my makeup."

I raise my brow in a skeptical stare. "Why? You did it to me."

He steps back, gaping at me. "True, but I had to stop you from finding out I was there in the first place because I knew it would look suspicious. I didn't want you believing I was the one who killed Jessica. I didn't do it. She was already dead when I arrived."

"How did you get into the apartment?"

He wipes his forehead with the back of a hand. "The door was unlocked so I let myself in. I immediately spied Ellinor passed out in a living room chair. The apartment was eerily quiet which was out of character for Jessica, who always had music on. I went straight to Jessica's bedroom where I spotted her on the floor. It was obvious at first glance that something was terribly wrong. Her head was at an odd angle and blood had pooled on the carpet next to her. I tried for a pulse but there was none."

"What did you do?"

"At first I was paralyzed with grief. Then I panicked, knowing how it would look if I was discovered standing over her. I blindly stumbled out of the apartment and wandered the city streets for who knows how long. Finally, I found myself outside of Jessica's and my favorite bar. I closed it down that night."

Tears fill his eyes. I have the urge to drape an arm around his shoulder, but instead I pluck a tissue off the nurse's station and hand it to him.

He wipes his eyes. "Sorry. I know this isn't exactly professional, but I can't help myself. I've been crying every day since Jessica died. I can't even think about it without breaking down."

"It's a terrible thing." I glance at the clock. "The staff meeting's about to begin. Can you make it?"

He crumples the tissue and tosses it in the trash. "I'll need a couple of minutes to compose myself so please let them know I'll be a few minutes late."

I agree and hurry off in the direction of the meeting room. Although the only testimony I have to collaborate Aaron's story is from a drunk woman, I want to believe he's being honest with me. But that has yet to be seen."

Chapter Twenty-Five

Ellie

Ellie sat across the table from Damien. She hadn't seen much of him in recent days and now that she was lying low in Roxbrough, it wasn't convenient for them to get together after a long day at work. At least that's what he told her. She had the distinct feeling their relationship was waning and would slowly dissolve, like ice in her water glass, until it had all melted away. The idea made her sad, but there was little she could do to recharge it, especially now that she was living in exile, preoccupied with her own survival.

Damien looked well and seemed pleased to be with her, but she suspected that was nothing more than an act.

"So how have you been?" she asked, eager to engage him in conversation.

"Fine. Just fine. And you?"

Of course, she had hoped he would tell her how much he missed her. How lonely he was without her. How he loved her. Instead, he sounded about as comfortable as she was miserable. At this rate, she'd never get around to asking what she wanted to know; do you want to be with me? "I'm all right. I've been through a lot lately."

The waitress came by and set platters on the table along with a basket of bread and butter.

"Um…" He reached for a slice of bread and pat of butter. "You sure have."

He seemed more interested in what side his bread was buttered on than in her predicament. "It's good seeing you."

"You, too."

If she were asked to describe his mood, she'd say nonchalant and casual. He didn't appear too concerned about her. "I asked you out to lunch today because I need to find out a few things about Hank."

He cocked his head. "Why? What does Hank have to do with anything?"

She had gone over the response to this question a dozen times, but she still didn't know what to share and what to hide. "Hank's become a friend of mine and he's helped me out on a couple of different occasions."

Suddenly Damien appeared interested. "Hank never mentioned anything to me."

"That's strange."

He leaned toward forward, elbows on table. "What did he do for you?"

"He came by the apartment one time…"

He stopped her with a hand on her arm. "I know. I'm sorry I didn't mention anything to you earlier, but I leant him the key so he could run by and get my phone, which I left behind one morning. Since you were at work when he went by, I didn't bother saying anything. I hope he didn't scare you."

Her mouth had dropped open and she had to take a second to recover before she said, "What? You gave him a key to my apartment? I can't believe this!"

"Did he stumble in on you? I screwed up, didn't I? I don't even know what to say…"

So, that explained how Hank had gotten into the apartment without forced entry…he had a key! Damn! She had an overwhelming desire to yell at Damien, call him a moron, but she swallowed the urge because she had a greater purpose here and didn't want to alienate him. "No, nothing like that…I don't like anyone having a key unless I authorize it. Please don't ever do that again without first running it by me." She wanted to ask for his key back, but since she had a favor to ask, this wasn't an opportune moment.

He looked sheepish. "I won't. I promise. So, what was Hank doing for you?"

"He gave me advice on a computer upload I needed to make on my accounting program and fixed the garbage disposal. I have another repair he could do, but I haven't been able to get ahold of him lately. Have you?"

Damien shook his head. "You know, I haven't spoken to him in a couple weeks. I've left him a message, but he hasn't returned it or been to his regular meetings. I was becoming worried about him."

"Yeah, me, too. Do you know how to reach him besides his cell phone? How about his address?"

"No. Hell, I don't even know his last name."

Since everyone goes by their first name in AA to protect anonymity, that was a quirk of the program. "How about where he works?"

"All I know is it's near 69th Street, but there are tons of mechanics in the area."

"Do you know any other way of contacting him?"

"No 'fraid not."

Sounded like she had reached a dead-end. "Do you have a picture of Hank?"

"Nah. He never wanted to have his picture taken. What do you want it for?"

Time to fess up. "To be honest with you, there's another reason I want to know about Hank. I wasn't sure I should tell you about this because I didn't want to interfere in your relationship until I was more certain, but Hank might have been in Jessica's apartment the night she was murdered."

Damien blanched. "What? Are you sure of that? Why would he be there?"

"I don't know, but Sarah would like any information you have about him."

"I'm still dumbstruck." Damien wiped his mouth and placed the napkin on the table. "It doesn't make sense. Why wouldn't he have told me about this?"

"Maybe he's covering something up?"

"Why would he do that? He seemed so helpful. Why he's the one who came up with the referral to Sarah and he seemed so interested in your therapy."

I raised my hands in question. "Perhaps there was an ulterior motive for his interest. Who knows."

Damien shook his head and his thick dark hair fell over his forehead. "Wow, that's pretty devious, but I guess it kinda makes some sense. Why that asshole!" He considered for a moment. "I have an idea. Assuming Hank's at the Monday morning meeting, I can sneak a photo of him on my cell. Would that work?"

"Sure, and if you can ply him for anything, that would be great. Since I know what he looks like, maybe you could send the photo to Sarah so she has a copy of it. I'll message her number to you. And, one last thing, please don't mention anything to Hank just yet. I don't want to alert him that we might be onto him."

"All right. But if you want me to keep a secret, I'll need to know one of yours." Damien cocked his head to the side in a boyish jester. "Where exactly are you staying right now? You're being so elusive."

She squared her shoulders against his charm. "I'm afraid I can't share that with anyone."

"I'm not just anyone. I'm your boyfriend."

She wasn't too sure of that. "Sorry. I promised Sarah I'd keep it to myself for now."

Damien's smile faded. "All right, if that's the way you want to play this." He looked at his cell and stood, "I better be getting back to the office. I'll give you a holler later," and hustled out the door.

He didn't even give her a hug goodbye. From her perspective at that moment, later looked like a long time off.

"I didn't get much of anything from Damien, although he told me he hasn't seen Hank recently. He promised to take a photo of Hank if he showed for the morning meeting. See if he sent you a text."

Sarah rummaged around in her purse and extracted her cell. She pressed a few buttons, stared at the screen and immediately turned as white as the office wall. "Oh!"

Ellie sat forward on the edge of her seat. "What is it? What's the matter?"

Sarah's hand trembled as she studied the photograph. "Oh my god," she sputtered. "I can't believe this."

Her behavior was worrying. "You can't believe what? Answer me, Sarah. What's bothering you?"

Sarah slowly raised her eyes to meet Ellie's, but where Ellie's were probably lined with concern, Sarah's held pure, unadulterated fear. "I know this man."

"Who is he?"

Sarah looked at the screen again, as though she was trying to reassure herself she wasn't mistaken before she said anything. "His name is Drew Cramer."

Ellie raised her hands in confusion. "Drew who?"

"I left that man hanging from a tree limb a few years ago after he tried to murder me."

Now it was Ellie's turn to gasp. "What?"

"You don't need the whole story right now...especially since this is your session, but this man is a cold-blooded psychopath. I have no doubt that he could be your murderer."

Ellie sat back, still a bit confused and unnerved, but reassured by the fact Sarah was onto something. "You mean to tell me he's done this before?"

"Yes, that's right."

"Who'd have thought? He seemed so helpful and friendly."

"Helpful?" Sarah asked. "I remember you mentioning that Damien had gotten my name through a friend. Was Hank that friend?"

"Yep. He's the one."

"That kind of thing is typical of Drew. He's been known to manipulate things so he has control over the situation and can elicit knowledge. It's pretty obvious he didn't want you to remember what happened with Jessica without his knowing it." She bit her lip "By manipulating Damien, he could keep a handle on what you recalled and who knew about it. Is it possible he suggested Damien ask you out in the first place? I wouldn't be surprised."

Ellie's eyes welled. So Hank might have encouraged her relationship with Damien. It confirmed what she believed, that she wasn't attractive enough to meet a man without help. If it wasn't for girlfriends matching her up, or her mother finding the biggest nerd, she would never have had a date in the first place.

Sarah must have sensed her misery. "I'm not saying Damien wasn't interested in you, I'm only speculating about Drew's motives."

"Yeah...sure..." She said, unsure. "So, where do we go from here?"

"You go back to the safe house for now. I don't want you to be anywhere Drew can find you." Sarah still looked sickly pale, which wasn't reassuring. "I have to consider where to go with this. I know of a way to smoke Drew out, but he's a dangerous character and I don't want to put anyone at risk. Let me consider this over the next couple of days and we'll talk again. In the meantime, keep your eyes open for anyone who might be following you...and better yet...stay away from familiar places as much as you can."

"How about leaving here?"

Sarah stood and grabbed her purse. "Right. There's a rear exit to this building. I'll drive you to the closest subway station. From now on, we'll communicate by phone and only meet when we absolutely have to, taking all precautions. Drew has outwitted me before, I'm not about to let him outwit me again. We'll have to play it safe."

They headed toward the door, but Sarah stopped and surveyed the hall before she allowed Ellie to emerge from the office. "Come this way." She directed Ellie to the stairwell instead of the elevator. "I'm going to do everything in my power to protect you, but you will have to do your part to protect yourself."

"Okay, I promise." But she wasn't sure what that meant...nor certain if she could manage it.

She left the clinic with Sarah, a pit as large as a dragon fruit's in her stomach. Even securely strapped into Sarah's Prius, she found herself clenching her fist and grinding her jaw. A tension headache lurked closely behind her left eye. By the time Sarah dropped her off at the Chestnut Street station, with a hug and another warning, she was already exhausted. She sprinted to the train, wary of any man who passed her by, and was relieved when it arrived without incident at her stop, where she hopped a bus to Ridge Avenue.

She trotted back to the safe house from the bus stop, relieved to be inside and out of harm's way. Although the house didn't feel like home, at least it was anonymous, which her apartment would never be as long as Hank was free. Sarah had agreed to contact the police with the new information, which was a relief since they had already discounted her earlier statements and probably wouldn't take her more seriously now. Having trouble sitting still, even to watch tv or read a book, she had no choice but to wait and see what Sarah proposed next.

Ellie retrieved a bottle of milk from the refrigerator and poured herself a glass. She rarely drank milk unless it was in coffee, but she suddenly wanted the succor only milk could offer. Nothing in her world seemed safer than standing in a stranger's kitchen drinking a glass of cold comfort. As a matter of fact, nothing seemed safe at all.

She pictured Sarah as the color drained from her face and a bolt of anxiety surged through her. Whoever this Drew was, he scared the living daylights out of Sarah, which wasn't reassuring. What had this man done before? And what was he capable of doing now?

The phone rang. She grasped it, but didn't recognize the number. She wasn't about to answer the phone to a stranger after what she had learned.

Playing back the voicemail, she heard a muffled voice say, "Hello, Ellie. If you believe you'd heard the last from me, I hate to disappoint you." A sinister laugh. "You know more than you should which makes you an extremely dangerous gal where I'm concerned. It would be wise if you were to keep what you know to yourself, but if you don't, I promise I'll hunt you down. You have no idea what I can do to you. Remember, you can't hide from me. No matter where you go, I will find you."

A click, and the caller hung up.

Her skin crawled and she could barely catch her breath. This message, compounded by Sarah's reaction, convinced her his threats were real. Her life was in danger. She couldn't hide in Roxborough forever, but she had nowhere else to go.

Chapter Twenty-Six

Sarah

After leaving Ellie at the Subway stop, I return to my office to cancel all my afternoon appointments. I need time to figure out a way to assist Ellie. Knowing Drew, I had better come up with a scheme sooner, rather than later. I have to think fast and plan well. There's no room for error.

As I leave a message for my five o'clock, Sam sticks his head through the door. "Have a few?"

I wave him into the room.

Once I finish with my call, I point to a chair. "What's going on?"

"I came by to ask you the same question. I know you have Ellie in a safe place, but you can't keep her there forever. Have you spoken to the police?"

"Yes, but without much luck. They're still saying they have no concrete evidence to support Ellie's contention that Jessica was murdered and they aren't giving much credence to the statement of a drunk woman who originally didn't even know she was in the apartment, let alone that she might have heard the murder and seen the murderer."

"That's certainly a stretch."

I debate how much to share with Sam, but decide it's best to be transparent. I don't want him to interfere in or abort my plans, but he's been supportive so far and I can't see why that would change. "Ellie presented me with a picture of this Hank fellow and it turns out, he's the same A-hole who almost killed me."

Sam's eyes open wide. "What?"

"He's the jerk who tried to toss me off a hill over the East River Drive."

He wears a skeptical expression. "That's quite a coincidence."

155

"Not really. He's the one who suggested Ellie see me in the first place. Which isn't surprising, considering the source."

"Why would he do that?"

"It was a set-up. He works with her boyfriend in AA and I'm sure he pumped Damien for as much as he could gather without looking suspect. And, on top of that, he managed to secure a key to her apartment. He's positioned himself perfectly to keep an eye on developments."

Sam narrows his eyes. "Why that SOB. So, he manipulated the entire thing in his favor. How'd he pull that one off?"

"My guess is he tailed her to an AA meeting in the first place. From there it probably wasn't too much of a stretch to find someone to do his bidding. He's a master manipulator."

"And it worked?"

"Sure sounds like it did. This tells you most of what you need to know about Hank, who's real name is Drew. He's as successful a con artist as I've ever encountered. Which makes him a serious threat."

Sam leans forward, elbows on thighs, hand under chin, in rapt attention. "So what's your plan of attack?"

Good question. I wish I had a simple answer. "I have an idea but I'm not sure it will work and I don't want to put anyone else at risk."

"Okay. What is it?"

"I hate to sound cryptic, but let's just say I know someone who might be able to smoke this guy out."

"Who is it?"

I watch Sam closely to gage his reaction, reassured when he barely blinks. "An old client of mine."

"And this client, is willing and able to assist you?"

"I don't know yet, nor do I know if it's a good idea to include her in this scheme. Drew is unpredictable. Even though he believes he's in love with her, I'm not sure what he'll do if he finds out she betrayed him by working with me."

"Mmmm. I see your problem. You don't want to complicate an already complicated situation, but you also don't want to leave Ellie exposed. Be careful in whatever you decide. Consider your professional responsibility to both these clients. And even though I have no input where your private practice client is concerned, I am responsible for Ellie's well being. Take that into consideration."

"I understand. I'll be scouring my conscience for what feels right to me."

Sam rises and and goes over to the window over Spruce Street. Turning his back to me, he gazes out at the buildings beyond. I stare at his back, afraid of what he's thinking. When he turns back to me, there's so much love in his eyes, it causes me to squirm.

"You're an amazing woman, Sarah. I can't tell you how much I admire your toughness and commitment. I..." and there he falters.

Uncomfortable with where this might go, I interrupt. "I'm not doing anything more than any other conscientious therapist would do. I'm sure you would do the same thing in my place."

"I'm not so certain of that. You're taking real risks here, not only with your license, but with your life. I don't know if I would have the fortitude to face those challenges." He strides over to me.

I flash him a palm to stop him. "Please...I'm still not ready to make any promise to you. It's not that I haven't been considering what to do, but with all that's been going on here, I haven't had a chance to give it my undivided attention. I need more time..."

"I know that. But don't put me on the back burner for long. I can't handle much more of this. It's eating me alive."

The stricken look in his eyes devastates me. I want to reach out to him, to take him in my arms, but I can't. "I know...I know it's not fair to you. It would be easier to simply give you the go ahead right now, but I don't want to lean on you out of fear or confusion. I want to do this of my own accord. When I've accomplished what I need to, I'll be more able to make a decision from a place of inner strength, not a place of fragility."

His shoulders slump, but he holds his head high and his eyes never leave mine. "I respect that and I'll do my best to be there for you, but I can't promise for how long. You can't expect me to wait forever."

Although my heart is aching, I say, "Of course not."

He pivots abruptly on his heels and begins to exit the room, but halts at the door. "No matter what you decide to do, please be careful, Sarah. You know you're dealing with a bad character. Take care of yourself...and take care of Ellie."

I salute him. "I'll do my best, boss."

He exits the room, and I know I won't hear anything other than professional advice from him from this moment on, leaving me with a deep well of emptiness inside where anticipation and joy had once resided. I stay at my desk for the longest time, nursing my wounded soul, until realizing how much time has passed and how much closer I am to my impending dance with the devil. While Sam is a lovely diversion, I have to figure out the best way to deal with Drew.

Or he will preempt me and figure out a way to deal with Ellie first...before dealing with me.

I navigate the circular driveway and park in front of Lara's lovely home, the house I have coveted for years. I ring the bell and, after a long silence, Lara answers the door and shows me into the foyer. The expression on her face is undisguised concern. "Are you okay? What's going on? It's not like you to take an afternoon off."

Behind her I can see Dicky playing with a video game in the family room, too busy to even acknowledge me. She follows my stare. "I managed to quiet him down for a bit. We better take advantage of the time we have. Let's have a cup of coffee while we talk."

In her recently renovated kitchen with the large center island, the orange Deco-style refrigerator and the most high tech six burner gas stove I have ever encountered, she pours us both a cup of coffee and we carry our cups to the glass and chrome kitchen table.

She takes a sip. "So what's going on?"

"Work problems, but I don't really want to burden you with them. I just needed to be in a safe place to think things through. I hope I'm not bothering you. I plan to take my laptop up to your guest room."

"First of all, you're never a burden. You're my favorite sister..."

"Your only sister."

"That's beside the point. You know I adore you."

"I know, but last time I used you as a sounding board, it wasn't helpful to either of us.

"Sorry about that. I felt awful about letting you down. It's just that I don't have all the answers, but if you need me to listen to a problem, I can certainly do that."

"You sure of that?"

Lara sips her coffee. "Yes, I am."

My hand trembles ever so slightly as I lower my cup. "I'm going to have to do something way out of the realm of normal therapeutic operating procedure and I'm wondering if I should do it."

"Okay," Lara says after a long pause, "lay it on me."

And I did.

Even though Lara isn't exactly enthusiastic about my plan, she concurs that it might be the only viable option to save Ellie's life. While I would have loved her blessing, my main goal for the afternoon is to clarify and solidify my plan before I proceed, and it doesn't hurt to inform her of my strategy in case things go awry. I would hate to have her find out after the fact, which would be devastating. As it is, she won't be totally shocked.

I leave her house knowing what I have to do next. Once in a safe place away from Lara's house, I pull the car to the curb, rummage in my purse for my cell and dial Rachel. The phone rings a number of times before the voicemail kicks in. I leave a message, telling her I need to speak with her as soon as possible.

Afterwards, I sit, gripping the steering wheel and staring out the window at the road ahead, wondering where it all might lead.

I answer the phone on the fourth and final ring. "Hello," I say, breathlessly, having run in from the patio.

"Sarah, you called? Is anything wrong?" Rachel asks.

Just like her to worry even before there's cause. "I have a proposal for you, but I'd understand if you're not interested in it."

I hear a gulp on the line. "Does this proposal have anything to do with our mutual friend, because I've been worried sick ever since I heard Drew was free on parole."

I try to calm myself so I won't sound frightened or frantic. "Actually it does. But before I say anything, how are you doing?"

"I was doing fine until I heard about Drew. Since then I'm a tight ball of nerves. I've been driving Evan crazy, but I don't know what to do. I don't sleep, I'm startled by the slightest noise and I'm skittish about everything. In other words...I'm a mess."

Exactly what I expected. "I can sympathize with you. You're in a terrible situation with him on the loose. That's exactly why I called."

"All right. Lay it on me, Sarah. What is this proposal of yours."

"You better sit."

"Uh oh." Again I hear the sound of swallowing. "Am I in trouble?"

"Lets hope not." I wipe perspiration off my brow, fortify myself. "I need you to help me draw out Drew so we can take him off the streets again."

"Oh my God, I'd love to help you, but I don't have the courage."

"I know how frightened you must be with him on the lam, because sooner or later he's going to figure out where you are. You know as well as I do that it's only a matter of time." I pause and let that sink in. "He's already broken into my office looking for your file and he's followed me home, probably more than once. So far I've been able to keep the file hidden, but it would only take one slip on the part of your parents or friends for him to gain information...and maybe even access."

"Damn," she moans. "Jesus. What the hell am I going to do?"

"I've been on pins and needles ever since he was paroled. We both know how dangerous, even deadly, he is. I can't imagine either of us will be safe until we find a way to put him back behind bars."

Her voice wobbles when she asks, "So, what's your plan?"

"Hold on. I want to get out of the car before I say anything more. I don't trust he hasn't found a way to bug it." I slide out of my seat and make my way to a shady area under a tree. I scan the area closely to be certain no one suspicious is hanging around. "Okay, this is a long story so sit tight." I go into detail describing Ellie's, alias 'Elaine's, circumstances. I finish my story to a deafening silence. "Are you still there? Are you okay?"

It takes a good twenty seconds before she answers, "Yeah, I'm all right. Stunned, but okay."

"The good news is you're not alone. He would love to get his hands on Elaine too, if only to break her neck. So, now there's three of us who have a stake in removing him from civil society."

"What good does that do?"

"Don't they say there's power in numbers. If we all band together, we might be able to find a way to entrap him before he's able to get to any one of us...you know, the best defense is a good offense...right?"

"So how do you propose we do this?"

I don't have a more appropriate metaphor. "I'm afraid we'll need to use you as bait."

She gasps. "I was afraid of that."

"You're the only one who can draw him out. Without your help, I don't know what else I can do to protect either Elaine...or you."

"I...I...don't know. I can't do this...The idea of being near him is petrifying. I'm having stomach spasms just thinking about it. I'm sorry, h really I am."

Although disappointed, I can empathize with her feelings. "Will you please reconsider this before you make a final decision? Right now, you're in as much danger as Elaine, and I don't want either of you hurt, but I don't have a better solution. The police say we need more evidence to put Drew away. My idea is to give them that evidence."

"Oh, God. Oh, God. Oh God," she repeats over and over again. "I don't know…"

"Your hesitation makes sense to me and I don't want you to do anything if it's too much for you. I'm just asking you to give it more consideration. If you can come up with a better solution, I'm all ears, but so far, this is the best I can do. Please, consider it, Rachel, and give me a call back in the next day or two with your answer."

"I better go. The baby's crying." After a long hesitation, which gives me the impression she's gotten off the line, I'm about to end the call when I hear her whisper, "Okay. I'll think about it, Sarah, and I'll get back to you once I make up my mind."

"That's all I ask."

Long after Rachel hangs up the phone, I sit behind the wheel of my car and weigh the enormity of my request. If she agrees to do what I ask, she will be putting her life on the line. This might all turn out to be a deadly exercise in futility…or the only option we have for stopping Drew from creating more havoc, destruction, or even death in his wake.

Only time…and Rachel's cooperation…will tell which it will be.

Later that evening, the phone jangles. I answer. Rachel's on the other end of the line.

"I'm in, Sarah. I've struggled with this decision all day and it only feels right to go ahead and do it. I'll do whatever it takes to capture that A hole."

While I'm relieved for all our sakes, as her therapist I have to ask, "Are you sure about this? You do realize what you might face?"

"I do."

"And you did talk it over with Evan?"

"No, I didn't. I know he'd be opposed to my doing this, but I need to do it for my own peace of mind. I'll never have a sense of safety and security in my life until I know this criminal is off the street."

"But what will this do to your relationship with him if he finds out?"

"By the time he finds out, I'll be a statistic anyway. If this succeeds, I will never tell him I was involved in it. Lips sealed...okay?"

"Okay. If you're certain you want to proceed, the next step is for you and 'Elaine' to meet. I'll be speaking with her tomorrow and we'll make arrangements. It's important you get to know one another. I'll call you after I speak with her."

"Good night. Sleep tight." The line goes dead.

The last thing I'll do is sleep tonight, knowing what is about to unfold.

Chapter Twenty-Seven

It was easy to spot Rachel outside the Arch Street entrance to the Reading Terminal Market. She looked exactly as described: petite with her long red hair and green eyes. Dressed in jeans, a royal blue knit top, and expensive looking sandals, she was a knockout. Next to her, anyone might be awkward, but since that described Ellie's typical state of mind, she felt more clumsy than usual. Rachel's warm smile and unexpected hug quickly put her at ease.

"Hi, sister in crime."

With litter all around, Ellie quipped, "More like sister in grime," trying to lighten the mood.

With a nervous chuckle, Rachel looked around. "Could we go inside? I don't hang around Philly too often since...well, since my troubles with Drew. I'd like to get off the street."

"I'm not sure Reading Market is any better than Arch Street. Perhaps we should have arranged a more out of the way location."

"Yeah, you're probably right, but while I'm in town, I was dying for a DiNic's roast pork sandwich and an Amish whoopie pie. They're the best. Lets find some food and an out of the way corner."

Ellie followed Rachel into the market, wondering how she maintained that trim figure with her dietary proclivities. If she ate what Rachel did, she'd be ten pounds heavier.

They both picked out sandwiches, although Ellie reluctantly passed up the whoopie pie, and wandered toward the rear of the market. Packed with people, Reading Market pulsed with the mid-day crowd. At counter after counter of delicious looking goodies, they had to detour around long lines of workers on lunch break or tourists from the nearby historical sites. Finally, after snaking their way through the crowded aisles, Rachel led her behind a cheese counter to a few isolated tables.

"I've been a regular here long enough to know all the nooks and crannies." They placed their food on the table and took seats. "Sarah told me a bit about you so I'd recognize you, but she didn't want to share too much with patient privacy and all. I'm glad we're getting a chance to meet before the main event."

Ellie giggled nervously at the inappropriate allusion. It would be more of an encounter...maybe even a clash or skirmish...than an event. "I'm not sure where to begin except to tell you that I knew Drew as Hank. He was my boyfriend's sponsor in AA. We both believed he was a good guy. Now that we know differently, we both feel taken in by him."

"You're not alone. Drew's not only a master criminal, but he's also a master of disguise. I don't know how much Sarah told you about my situation, but he was successful at fooling me as well as a friend of mine. Unfortunately, she never knew what hit her."

"That makes me feel a little less naïve and stupid for letting him into my life. How did it happen to you?"

She spent the next hour munching on amazing food and listening to equally amazing stories of Drew's shenanigans. By the end of that hour, she felt safe enough with Rachel to face what they had to do together. And she sensed Rachel felt the same way about her. Ellie had questioned the necessity of meeting Rachel ahead of time, but now she saw the wisdom in it. Knowing and trusting one another could be crucial to the outcome of their strategy. This was Sarah's way of readying them for their trial by fire the only way she could.

Fifteen minutes later, as they were winding their way through the crowd to the Arch Street exit, Rachel grabbed Ellie's arm. "He's here," she whispered.

Rachel's reaction caught Ellie by surprise. She searched near and far, but could see little with the crush of people and activity. Was Rachel really sensing Drew's presence, or was she merely reacting out of fear? Ellie didn't know, but why take a chance. "What should we do?"

"I prepared for this." Rachel reached into her pocket, extracted her cell phone and spoke into the receiver. "Meet me right outside of the Arch Street exit in five." Then she grabbed Ellie's arm and whisked her toward the door. "My husband's a couple blocks away and will be right over. He doesn't know anything about what we're doing so please don't give me away. I told him I was having lunch with an old friend."

Ellie lurched alongside Rachel. "Of course not."

Within minutes of exiting the building a cab roared over to the curb with Rachel's husband, Evan, in the backseat. They jumped in. "Take us on a roundabout ride to Pennsylvania Station. I'm trying to lose someone," Rachel said to the driver.

"Okay miss...you asked for it." The cabbie took off at a fast clip, veering up and down city streets, weaving in and out of traffic, making sudden turns and, after twenty minutes, pulling into Penn Station. Rachel and her husband, Evan, exited the cab and gave the driver directions and a few dollars to take Ellie back to Roxborough.

While she tried to pay them back for their generosity, they refused to take the funds. She left Rachel with a good impression, but no matter how positive she felt, she wasn't looking forward to the next time they'd meet.

The next day Ellie met with Sarah at the door to the safe house.

"I must have circled the block ten times to make sure I wasn't being followed. This abundance of caution thing has it's limits," Sarah said, climbing the stairs to the second floor condo.

"Tell me about it." Ellie let Sarah into the condo through a solid wood door. Inside, the living room had a contemporary look with white walls and oak floors. "I made some coffee." She led Sarah into the kitchen with ceramic tiled floors, composite countertops, and white *melamine* cabinets.

Sarah took a seat on a stool by a counter. "I was a nervous wreck the whole way over thinking I might lead Drew to you. I must have made thirty turns to throw anyone behind me off track. Try doing that in mid-day traffic."

"What a headache this is. I can't wait until it's over."

"Ditto."

Ellie poured two cups of steaming coffee and joined Sarah at the counter. "So, what's the plan, ma'am."

Sarah took a sip and sighed. "Great java." She placed the cup on the countertop before continuing. "First thing we have to do is make sure Drew is alerted to Rachel's whereabouts on the day we designate. Any idea what day will work for you?"

Since she had taken leave from work, she had an easy answer. "Any day. You name it."

"Rachel would prefer to do it a week from Monday since that's the day she typically takes her child to daycare for a couple hours in order to run errands. How's that work for you?"

"Does that give us enough lead time to let Drew know?"

"It's tight, but we can always do a dry run if he fails to show."

"So what's next?"

"I already threw together a couple of fake files for Rachel. To be safe, I'll leave one in the office, the other at home. He'll probably visit one of those sites within the next week."

Ellie shivered and rubbed my arms. "Creepy."

"More than you realize. I've been living with this guy on the loose for the last few months knowing that he would be pursuing me to gain insight on Rachel. It's been horrible."

The more Ellie heard, the less she liked, but there was only one way out and that was in. "If you want me to leave something in my apartment, I can do that, too. He has a key so there's every reason to believe he might snoop around in there."

"We could leave a note saying that we're meeting with Rachel on Monday at...what...one in the afternoon?"

"One would work. But where?"

"Rachel has a friend with a rental house in Allentown that's uninhabited at the moment. Maybe you can mention in the note that Rachel will be there around thirty minutes early to take pictures of the house for rent. That way he'll know she'll be there alone. I can also mention that in my files."

"Sounds ingenuous."

"I hope clever enough to fool him. The one thing on our side is his determination to see Rachel. He might be more easily mislead. Fingers crossed."

"From what you've said it's going to take more than crossed fingers and voodoo to stop this maniac. I can only hope you're right about power in numbers." Because otherwise, we all might be out of luck.

Chapter Twenty-Eight

Sarah

Eager to leave the hospital on time Monday morning, I rush down the hallway at a jog and pass Sam on his way back to his office. He grasps a file closer to himself so its contents won't spew out all over the corridor. "Whoa there, Sarah. Where are you off to in such a hurry."

I clasp my purse, acting as though I am afraid of dropping it, in the hope he doesn't notice the handgun outlined in the cloth bag. I failed to mention to Sam the specifics of my plan because I didn't want him to try and talk me out of it. It isn't exactly foolhardy, but it also isn't the safest and smartest thing I'd ever done considering I am about to confront the man who tried to kill me once already. If it doesn't go as planned, he might succeed this time around. "I have a doctor's appointment this morning. Can't be late."

I try to step past him, but he stops me with a hand on my arm. "I've been feeling like you're avoiding me lately, Sarah. I'd would like to speak with you soon. When do you have time for me?"

Good question. I'm not crazy about having to deal with him with everything else going on, but I can't postpone the inevitable forever. "I'm late. Can we talk about this when I return?"

He looks exasperated. "You can't put me off indefinitely. We need to discuss what matters..."

I manage to maneuver away from him. "Sure...sure. You're right. I promise I'll stop by your office later to establish a time, but right now I can't delay. See you," I say over my shoulder as I sprint off in the direction of destiny. Quickly forgetting all about Sam in my obsession with the near future.

Ellie waits on the stoop for me. She points at her watch as I pull into the parking lot in front of her unit.

"We're already a few minutes late. We better go." She slides into the driver's seat and, as soon as she belts in, I back out and hit the

169

accelerator. "Sorry, I was held up a few minutes longer than I planned." I careen onto Media Rd. and make a sharp, squealing turn onto Baltimore Pike. "Sit tight. I'll try to make up for lost time. I want to be there no later than 12:15." I weave in and out of traffic to Route 476 North toward Allentown.

Ellie sits in silence for the longest time and I'm too busy driving to disrupt her thoughts. Finally, she turns to me. "I'd almost relinquished hope he'd find the note, but I believe he was in my apartment yesterday."

"Good, because I never had the sense he found those files I left for him. What makes you so sure he was there?"

I catch sight of Ellie kneading her hands. "I left the note on a table with a paperweight on top and the paperweight had been moved ever so slightly."

"How'd you figure that out?"

"I put a couple of dots on the paper around the edge of the paperweight so I could tell."

"Smart. So, it sounds like we might have our guy today..."

Ellie grabs my arm and I swerve. "Watch out!"

"Sorry, Sarah, but I'm scared to death. What if he has a gun? He might shoot us before we have a chance to nab him."

"If you're not up to this, let me know right away so I can alert Rachel. No use starting something we can't finish."

Ellie quiets and stares out the window. "I'm frightened, that's all. I have no choice but to go forward with this if I want to live a full life. Now that I know whodunit I have no doubt he'll be gunning for me. Without police protection, I'm a dead duck anyway. I can't see there's any other option." Her voice trembles when she speaks.

"My goal is to get this done quickly and safely. I don't want anyone hurt, even Drew." With a straight stretch of road in front of me and lighter traffic, I floor the accelerator pedal. "Let's get this over with before either of us has a chance to bow out."

We arrive in Allentown at 11:54, which is good because I have trouble locating the two story clapboard house on Main Street. While you might think it would be easy finding anything on Main Street, with my limited knowledge of Allentown, I manage to get turned around a bit after my GPS takes me the convoluted route...of course. Finally, I locate our destination. It's now 12:05. I park and point at the grey boxy house where Rachel awaits Drew's arrival. "That's it."

Turning toward Ellie, I am met with wide brown eyes. She places a hand over her chest. "I can barely breathe right now."

"Imagine how Rachel feels. I better text her that we're here. I told her to leave if I didn't text her before 12:15." I pluck the phone from my purse, but my hands tremble so much it's difficult to hold it stable and it keeps shifting when I try to type in the message. Lucky for *Siri*, I was able to speak it. "Rachel, we're outside the house. As soon as Drew enters, we'll be on our way in. Hang in there. We're with you."

Every minute we anticipate Drew's arrival seems like an hour, but 12:30 finally arrives. We breathlessly wait, eyes glued on the house, but we don't have to wait for long. Within a couple minutes, a man in a black hoody, drawn closely around his face, steps out from behind a bush, slithers over to the front door and jimmies the lock.

"We're on." I dial 911 on my cell phone and report a break-in at 547 Main Street. The operator tries to keep me on the phone, but I start say something and hang up as though we've been cut off. With the gun sheltered in the palm of my hand, I lead Ellie to the house. I try the front door, but much to my chagrin, Drew locked it from the inside. "No problem," I whisper. "I told Rachel to leave a window open in the rear in case he locked the door."

Ellie follows me around back. We jiggle the back door, but it too is locked. I quickly locate the window left ajar. "Hold onto this." I hand my gun to Ellie–who holds it away from her body and gazes at it as if it were on fire.

"Do you know how to shoot this thing?"

"My father taught me as a kid," I hiss out of the side of my mouth as I place both my hands under the pane and try to lift it using all my strength. It barely budges. I make a second attempt. The longer this takes, the greater the danger Rachel faces. Suddenly a scream fills my head.

Electric energy bolts through me. "I'll need your help!"

Ellie stares at me as though she doesn't speak the language. The gun quivers in her hand.

Another scream. I grab the gun from her and place it on the ground. "I'll take this side of the window, you take that one and we'll lift it together."

Wide-eyed, she nods her understanding. We station ourselves side by side with ours hands under the windowpane. "Now!" She grunts as we try to raise it. With the force of four hands, it moves upwards enough that I can shimmy inside. "Wait here. I'll get in and open the back door for you."

I scoop up the gun, give it to her and lift one leg over the sill. With a bit of a maneuver, I shimmy forward, tuck my head and shoulders into the house and squirm my torso inside. Sliding my other leg in proves the simple part. Once inside, I let Ellie in and retrieve my firearm. "Okay, lets head upstairs."

After unlocking the front door, we tiptoe our way up the stairs. About halfway, Rachel screams again. With pounding heart and sweaty palms, I grab for Ellie's hand and leap the rest of the stairs to the landing. Passing a couple of empty rooms, I come upon Rachel standing cornered in the back bedroom with Drew pressed against her.

I raise my gun and aim it at Drew. "Turn around slowly, Drew," I snarl. "I have a gun aimed at you."

Drew freezes. "Oh, it's you. What an unpleasant surprise."

The sound of his voice and the scent of his familiar cologne, cause my blood pressure to spike even before he turns to face us.

He grabs Rachel, pivots around and places her between us. "What good is that gun to you now, Abrams?"

"Damien!" Ellie gasps.

I look at Drew and back at Ellie, confused. "You said the killer was Hank. I saw the picture…"

Ellie is wide-eyed. "He sent you the picture…not me. I never saw it."

"But you identified Hank in Jessica's apartment…"

She shakes her head. "I was wrong."

"Shows you what denial can do."

Drew sneers. "Cut out the psychobabble and move out of my way."

I glance over at Ellie as if to say 'do as he tells us', but her eyes are fixed on him.

With one swift move, she shouts, "You son of a bitch," and lungs for Drew.

The shock of the sudden movement must have thrown him off-balance because he loses his hold on Rachel for a split second, enough time for her to spring out of Ellie's way. Ellie flings herself at Drew with all her weight and shoves him so hard he staggers backwards against the wall.

As he straightens, I point the gun at his head. "Don't move or I'll shoot."

Drew lifts his hands in front of his face. "Okay…okay. Don't shoot."

"Hold him," I shout.

Ellie takes ahold of one arm and Rachel the other. They both hold on tightly as planned.

I give Ellie a signal with my head. "Place the handcuffs on him."

Drew turns suddenly and violently shakes loose the hands holding him. He pushes past the two women and starts toward me. I am about to compress the trigger, when Ellie sticks her foot out and trips him. He crashes to the floor with a loud thud. Ellie tosses herself across his back and Rachel throws herself over his legs, encircling them with her arms and pinning him in place.

I point the gun at his head. "Don't you dare move one muscle! I will shoot, damn you!"

"You okay?" Ellie asked Rachel.

Rachel is holding onto his legs. "I won't let this Son of a Bitch get away again!"

"I have him covered and I'll shoot if he makes one false move. Go ahead," I said. "Cuff him."

Drew struggles, making it difficult to put cuffs on him. We all hear the sirens at the same time. I'm relieved the police are arriving before Drew can get away.

The impending police presence must have surprised Drew because he gives me a look I'll never forget. He flails his arms about in an attempt to reach for Ellie, but she has managed to maneuver around and sits squarely on his back, legs clamped on each side of his torso. She grabs his arms and pins them down. With Rachel securely applying pressure to his legs, he's trapped.

Drew eyes me with a smirk on his face. "What have you accomplished here, Abrams? The police don't have a thing on me except maybe a breaking and entering charge."

I smile back at Drew. "How about your assault on Rachel?"

"So...they can't keep me for long on that charge. I'll be back out on the street soon enough. And next time I'll make sure you don't get in my way!" He snarls at me.

A cold chill passes through me. I don't doubt his intent or his ability. All I can do is hope they put him away longer than they did the last time.

At the sound of police at the front door, relief blankets Ellie's face. At least we are safe...for now. Since none of us can move, I make my way to the door and scream down that the door is unlocked.

Drew watches, his face distorted into a macabre mask. "Bitches! Look at you. You're losers."

Even though every instinct urges me to move away from him, I step closer. "Actually, we're heroes today."

"And you're the loser," Ellie adds.

At that moment police rush into the room, guns drawn.

Later, we watch the police lead Drew away, then answer questions while a policewoman takes a report. Our job is finished for now. Outside, after a big group hug, I ask if anyone wants to debrief over a quick cup of coffee before heading back to our respective lives. Since Ellie isn't working, she's receptive to the idea, but Rachel has to pick up her daughter from daycare. We walk her the three blocks to her car, hug goodbyes, and find a coffee shop within easy walking distance. At the funky, little, corner shop, we carry our drinks to a table in the rear so we won't be disturbed.

As soon as we're seated, Ellie places her hand over her heart. "Oh my God, my heart's been beating so fast, it seems as if it will never slow to normal. I'm so relieved this is over with."

I concur. "That was the most exciting couple hours I've had in a long time, but it's the kind of excitement I can live without. I'm glad we all made it through in one piece."

"What now?" Ellie gingerly sips her steaming latte. "What will become of him?"

"If it's anything like last time, he's right, they won't be able to pin the murder charge on him. Even though you were a witness, the fact that you were in a blackout at the time of the murder and there are no other witnesses will work against us. And it probably doesn't help that you identified the murderer long after the event, while intoxicated...and it happened to be the wrong man."

"Yeah, I guess any decent lawyer would be able to drive a big rig through my testimony. What I can't get is how could I have believed it was Hank? That's so strange."

I chuckle. "The mind is amazing. You were so resistant to the idea it was Damien that your subconscious pulled one of it's mind-boggling tricks and substituted Hank in his place. The mind can be a magician of sorts. Smoke and mirrors."

"Unbelievable."

"But true."

"And the other thing that stumps me is Damien sending you his photo instead of Hank's. Why would he do that?"

I raise my palms in a gesture of confusion. "Perhaps it was a message of intimidation. Like he was thumbing his nose at me."

"Could be. Maybe he also figured if you believed he had murdered someone else and was on the prowl, you'd be motivated to set up a meeting with Rachel. You know, to warn her of the danger. Since his goal was to find her, he might have seen this as his way in."

"Hum... Makes sense. I mean...it worked, in a way, but not in the way he wanted it to."

"Yeah." We beam at one another.

My eyes never leave her face. This might be one of the last times I see Ellie. We have accomplished the goal she set out for herself and more, since she now has sober time under her belt and the backing of a sponsor and AA program. "So how are you doing after all this?"

"You know, it's strange. I've been in fear my entire life. Even though I might look large and in charge, I've always been a scared little girl underneath. I actually believe it may have been fear that caused me to drink in the first place. But today something snapped...and I don't know if I'll ever be that fearful again."

"It must seem like this has all happened suddenly, when you lunged at Drew, but you've been building toward this moment ever since I've known you. You took some big chances with your treatment and that took tremendous courage."

"Maybe, but it took until today for it to fully manifest. I wasn't sure I could even go through with the plan I was so frightened, but once I saw Damien...Drew...I could no longer stand the idea of being taken advantage of and made to feel useless. Suddenly, I was sick and tired of being treated like my mother treated me, like an ugly, awkward stepchild. I'd had enough!"

I could see the fire in her eyes. "You took a real risk confronting him the way you did."

"It didn't feel like I took a risk at all. I was so pissed...I had to do something or else I would never be right with myself."

I reached across the table and took her hand. "That's called self esteem."

She seemed to straighten, thrust her shoulders back, and looked taller than usual. "So that's what self esteem looks like."

"Not always so physical, but that's exactly what it was."

She beams again. "I like it."

And so do I. At this moment I know I can set her free. She has succeeded in every way possible and, thanks to Drew, has become the woman she always wanted to be. I can see it written all over her.

I arrive back at the office later than I expected, but I had called ahead to let everyone know. As I trot down the hall, tired but pleased with myself, I pass Sam's office. Since I have a few minutes and have put him off long enough, I poke my head through the door. "Have a few?"

He waves me in. "Sure. Take a seat."

I pull a chair up to his desk. He places the file he's working on aside. "So, what's going on?"

"First of all, I have to confess, I didn't go to the doctor today...I had an appointment to meet with Jessica's killer."

He opens his eyes wide. "You mean with Hank?"

"No, I mean Damien, Ellie's now ex-boyfriend, who's real name is Drew Cramer."

Sam wrinkles his brow. "That's convoluted. How did it turn out?"

"As good as can be expected. He's now in police custody, looking at breaking and entering and assault charges. Hopefully, the judge will be able to put him away for a few years."

"So did you catch him single-handedly?"

Here's where I have to confess to going over the line. I clear my throat "No, I recruited the help of Ellie and that other patient of mine from my private practice days."

He narrows his eyes. "You went ahead with it."

"I did. I couldn't have done this alone. I needed their help."

He rises from his seat and paces the floor. "Oh my, that's outside your job description."

I lower my head, waiting for the axe to fall. "Yeah, I know, but I didn't know how else to protect either of them. They were both in danger with Drew on the loose. He had killed three people that I know of, I didn't want him to kill anymore...especially not my patients."

Sam halts his pacing in front of me. "I know you're a highly involved and sincere therapist, but you really have overstepped your boundaries today. What would have happened if either of these patients had been hurt or killed? What would you have done?"

I don't know what to say. That had been a possibility, but I didn't allowed myself to consider the consequences because the outcome was so crucial to their survival. "But that didn't happen. They not only survived, but came out feeling stronger and safer, and in a much more secure place."

Sam places a finger under my chin and raises my head. "You know I'm going to have to write you up for this and I'm not sure what the board will do under the circumstances. I know your heart was in the right place, but you should have consulted with me before you did anything. I will do my best to explain to them what was going on and how much you wanted to protect your patients, but we'll have to leave the outcome to them."

"I understand." And I do. I knew my job was at risk when I got involved in this operation, I'm not at all surprised by his reaction. "I respect what you have to do...and I will take whatever comes my way with as much dignity as you have shown me the whole time I have worked under your direction."

With a hand on my shoulder and a look that could break a heart, he solemnly nods at me. I can see how much it hurts him to have to 'turn me in', but we both know he is doing the only thing he can. "I don't know if this is a bad time to bring up our relationship, but I don't know how much longer I can hold out without knowing how you wish to proceed. Have you given it any thought?"

Even though it's a bit awkward, I know how important this is to him. "I have."

I can sense him tense.

"Can you put your feelings about what I said aside long enough to give me your unbiased decision?"

"Yes, because I made the decision before all this happened today."

"Okay, let's have it."

"Can I preface this by saying that I think the world of you as a boss and as a man. You have always been patient and helpful and genuine with me and, for that, I will always be grateful."

"Uh oh," he says, "I feel the boom lowering."

I try to smile but my lips won't cooperate. "Every time I consider what I want, the Leonard Bernstein song from a play I did in High School, *West Side Story*, runs a loop in my brain." He has a stricken expression.

"You know: There's a place for us. A time and place for us...Why I'm telling you this is because I want you to know that even though this isn't the right time for us, I still believe there's a time and place for us..."

He removes his hand from my shoulder. "Are you sure your decision isn't being colored by my having to let the board know about today?"

"No, not at all." I shake my head vehemently. "This is not the right time to begin anything. You still have too much on your emotional plate and I have a lot on mine. We need to wait. I can't tell you exactly how long or why I feel this way, but I do, and I have to honor my sense of what's right for me."

He inhales deeply and lets it out with a huff. "Okay. Even though I'm not crazy about your decision, I will respect it as I know you respect mine. But I want to warn you, Sarah, I'm not about to give up on you. No matter what happens and how long it takes, you're worth any wait."

The smile I couldn't conjure earlier breaks out on my face. "I wouldn't expect anything less from you, because you, my dear friend, are an incredible man."

He lifts me to my feet and into his arms. "You know," he breaths into my hair, "with all I've been through lately I'm learning to accept that we don't always get what we want when we want it."

I pull back. "Acceptance. What do they say in AA…acceptance is the answer to all my problems today. When I am disturbed, it is because I find some person, place, thing, or situation—some fact of my life—unacceptable to me, and I can find no serenity until I accept that person, place, thing, or situation as being exactly the way it is supposed to be at this moment."

"Wow…" he laughs. "Where'd you get that?"

"Ellie gave me a Thank You card with that quote from the Big Book of Alcoholics Anonymous."

"I never expected what I said would cause you to go philosophical on me."

"Me either, but there you have it." I let him hug me one more time. "Now I better get back to work before I get into anymore deep water."

He ushers me to the door. "Yeah, me too. I have a deadline at five today for these month end reports. But don't you forget what I told you, because I won't."

I wink at him. "You don't have to worry about me, boss."

"I don't know about that, Abrams," he jokes. "I can't imagine what trouble you'll get yourself into next."

And neither can I.

The End

Don't miss out!

Visit the website below and you can sign up to receive emails whenever J. K. Winn publishes a new book. There's no charge and no obligation.

https://books2read.com/r/B-A-HKO-WWSJ

Connecting independent readers to independent writers.

Did you love *Night of the Shadow*? Then you should read *Out of the Shadow*[1] by J. K. Winn!

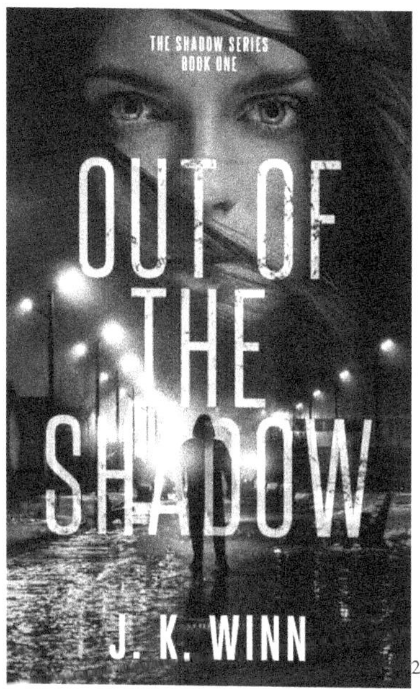

Two women. One goal. To uncover the truth no matter the cost.

A survivor of rape and her husband's murder, all Becca Rosen wants to do is move on with her life, but how can she when she's being stalked by a psychopath with an attitude---and an agenda. The police are no help because they're convinced, with her history of mental illness, Becca has faked the rape to get away with her husband's murder. On top of that, Becca has begun to have flashbacks of childhood abuse, possibly at the hands of the rapist. Not knowing where to turn, and feeling like she might go crazy again, Becca hires Psychologist, Sarah Abrams, to help her unearth who's behind the crimes of the past...and the present. Three men come into Becca's life around the same time.

---

1. https://books2read.com/u/mgZZv3

2. https://books2read.com/u/mgZZv3

While each of these men has his charms, Becca can't be certain whether any one of them is the perpetrator. Or could it be someone else? Together Becca and Sarah start on a course of hypnotherapy to discover abuser's identity. Will their work reveal the real killer before it's too late, or will Becca fall prey once again to this demented criminal?

If you like Out of the Shadow, check out Night of the Shadow, Shadow Series, Book 2 @ https://www.jkwinn.com

Like the layers of an onion, OUT OF THE SHADOW peels away personalities, motivations, underlying motives, and dark, long-hidden secrets that immerse a circle of people in a web of dangerous associations. **The conclusion is riveting, unexpected, and as satisfying as the rising psychological suspense which begins from the first page and ends with a bang.** D. Donovan, Midwest Book Review

This is such a terrific page-turner that I lost sleep on the three nights that it took for me to complete it. By the time I was two-thirds of the way through, I couldn't stand it any longer; **I cheated and checked out the ending--and I was blown away. I hope J. K. Winn writes her second novel very, very soon. Next time, I'll try hard not to start with the last chapter.** Debra Sponable, Nights and Weekends

Winn's suspenseful thriller thrusts readers into the intense trauma that may be Becca Rosen's psychological undoing...**A dynamic thrilling read for readers willing to focus on more than one perspective.** Kirkus Reviews

Also by J. K. Winn

Shadow Series
Out of the Shadow
Night of the Shadow

The Spirit Series
The Spirit Keepers
The Spirit Seekers
The Spirit Breakers: A Pueblo People's Mystery

Standalone
River of Desire
The Last Supper: A Short Story
Hold Back the Wind

About the Author

J K Winn has many stories to share. After years of working in the "real" world, she decided to reinvent herself in mid-life and pursue her love of story. Out of the Shadow is her first published novel, but she has one prior novel published in genre, and one play produced by the Actor's Alliance Festival in San Diego. Her poetry has been anthologized in, For the Love of Writing, by the San Diego Writer's Workshop in 2011. Her play, Gotcha!, was selected for a reading at the Village Arts Theater in Carlsbad, California, May 2012.

Look for her latest romantic action adventure, RIVER OF DESIRE.

She presently lives by the beach in San Diego County, California. Visit her at her blog authorjswinn.wordpress.com or on facebook.com/authorjswinn

www.ingramcontent.com/pod-product-compliance
Lightning Source LLC
Chambersburg PA
CBHW061526120726

48001CB00004B/1416